I0737263

TO DEFINE US

Jasmine Martin

THE
OCEAN DEEP

To Define Us by Jasmine Martin

Copyright © 2023

All rights reserved. No portion of this book may be reproduced in any form without permission from the publisher, except as permitted by U.S. copyright law.

For permissons: Alexishunter0921@gmail.com

ISBN: 978-1-957674-14-8

Published by The Ocean Deep Publishing
13833 Dumfries Rd., Manassas, VA 20112

Printed in the USA.

TO DEFINE US

Jasmine Martin

When the world is burning, everyone stops to stare—it's those who move that get remembered.

Ryker Alix Griffin wasn't a bystander. He wasn't one to stop and watch as the world burned—he kept going. The world was burning, and if he couldn't stop it—he sure as hell was going down with it, and no one in the world would be able to stop him.

This is the story of a boy—a boy who had wanted to help save people from the beginning. This is his story.

Chapter 1

"Third floor, sharp right." The mutter of floor directions covered by the loud blaring of alarms. Red lights flashed in the otherwise lightless bland and white halls. Footsteps echoed on the polished wooden floor of the hall.

A man calmly strolled through the tiresome halls, following his own directions in the unpleasant building he had snuck into not long before. A quiet hum escaped him as he skipped into a room, a file swinging in his hand, turning around the right corner. He flipped the lights on and revealed the organized room filled with files cabinets along the walls and a desk in front of him. Everything in the room had long been settled in their places except for the items that lined the desk edge. Imprints surrounding them in a permanent pattern where they had sat for way too long. Speçial personal objects that did not sit straight nor strategically.

"Interesting."

As he walked along the wall, running his fingers along the metal of the files, the man stopped at a cabinet labeled R-S. The drawer above was labeled O-Q and below was just the letter T. With a swift yank, one of the drawers came rolling open to reveal a multitude of sorted files. A smile emerged on the man's face as he looked at the organized manilla folders below him. He began to shuffle through them until he reached the section he was looking for.

"There you go buddy. Perfect." An overly cheery, and high, voice spoke. He slipped the file in between two others where it had lived for so long. It's dusty friends missing it since the moment it had been stolen by unworthy hands mere days before. *Right back where you belong, out of that villain's hands.*

With one final gentle glance at the other files, he pushed the file cabinet closed and turned to leave the room, making sure to lock up unlike the person who had fled the room sometime that night. He began the long walk down the hall when a soft ringing echoed out, a vibrating coming in the man's pocket. He continued to let a hum escape him, pulling his black phone from the pocket of his black cargo pants. He let the phone ring twice before answering the incoming call.

"Hello?"

"Alix! Where are you? I thought you said you would be home by eight?" A worried voice rang through the phone. The well-worn nickname that was used only by the speaker rang out more than the other words.

"Sorry little bird, I had to fix someone else's mistakes for them. I will be home soon."

"Is that a fire alarm?"

"Yeah someone just messed up on making their dinner in the staff room. We're clearing out of the building now because we have to, so I'll leave when they give the all clear." Ryker spoke into the phone. A smile found its home on his face as he descended through the staircase on his path outside. "Is there anything you need on my way home?"

"Ice cream?" There was a pause. "Also, are you seriously using the nickname from when we were kids? We aren't in elementary school anymore."

A soft chuckle escaped from Ryker as he exited an emergency exit door and into the cold night of Silvar Fall City. Goosebumps forming on his arms with the unusually cool breeze that hit him upon exit, the town wasn't usually this cold until later into winter. He sent a quick glance towards the surrounding civilian's that stared up at the building with wide eyes—they all had their coats pulled close to them and many glared at the building for forcing them into the cold night. Their attention fully caught by the offices, hoping there was an actual reason to be out here.

"Sorry. I'll be home in a few minutes, Gray."

Just before Ryker hung up with his final goodbye, Gray—Grayson—called out a request, "Rocky road please!"

"I told you we need the police here!" Ryker's head turned towards the voice of an angry man yelling at a police officer who was just trying to do his job. The poor officer had only been in the area when the building had been forced to evacuate. "Ever since that... that *villian* stole from us we have been having weird things happening in the building. No one can explain it! Until that *hero* can give us back our stuff we need protection!"

Ryker turned in his path just enough to walk right past the two at the edge of the sidewalk. He slipped his hand into his pockets, his fingers rubbing against a piece of paper which he carefully pulled out. It fell from between his fingers, but he didn't look back even as he heard a gasp and someone called out to him. He just kept moving.

~~

Ryker kicked the door to his apartment open, his hands were too full with the bags of treats he had gotten from the nearby supermarket to be helpful in the opening job. A smile sat on his face as he moved into the building, taking the first left into what had been declared the living space; it wasn't really a room to him if there were just counter spaces instead of walls. Such an open design worked well for the two residents.

The living room TV was on already, blaring the noise of a reporter talking right outside of an evacuated building. The apartment's resident rolled his eyes at the scene of people running back and forth behind the talker or just doing weird things as they attempted to be on live TV. Did they not recognize how stupid they would look for years to come?

"I'm home!" Ryker called out. He dropped the bags onto the faux granite countertops.

Real granite was too expensive for buildings in this part of town, but maybe that was the appeal of the place for people like Ryker. Since it hadn't taken much money to stay here the cheap look wasn't a horrible thing, if anything it made Ryker feel more at home than he did at other places. Plus, either himself or his roommate could pay for the place all by themself. Grayson has enough money from his parents to survive on and Ryker had been working since he was a teenager so he had enough to pay for it. Something that was his.

"What took you so long?" A voice replied from just outside of the room and beyond the view of the kitchen.

"Well I thought you would like other snacks than just ice cream," Ryker called out, pulling some of the items from the bags one at a time. Some chocolate, gummy bears, chocolate chip cookies, and even soda were pulled from the bags. The receipt for the items was quickly crumbled and tossed away once it was found at the bottom of the bag. "You being picky makes it difficult to choose things, Grayson."

Ryker turned as he heard approaching footsteps, his eyes landing on the apartment resident who decided now was the best time to make an appearance. He turned back towards the food as he spoke, "Careful about the step. It hasn't changed while I've been gone unless you changed that somehow, but I doubt it."

"Jerk," Grayson mumbled, "I know my way around our own apartment. This isn't somewhere new."

"You say that but you tripped on it yesterday then threatened to have it removed like it could be scared of you." Ryker teased. "It's an inanimate object, Grayson, it never moves."

Out of the corner of his eye Ryker could see Grayson arrive as he leaned on the counter, his longish copper hair covering his eyes as he did so. He tilted his head towards Ryker.

"What exactly did you get, Alix?" Grayson asked.

Ryker slid a tiny tub of ice cream to touch Grayson's hand before going back to emptying the rest of the items. If Grayson's smile could have grown then it definitely would have done so as he moved away from the counter; running his fingers over the drawers before coming to a stop at one. Ryker rolled his eyes, grabbing his own very tiny tub of ice cream, moving towards the drawer Grayson had left open.

"Hey, close the drawers if not for my sake then your own." Ryker called out as he grabbed a spoon from the drawer.

"But it's so much easier when you do it."

"Until I choose not to." Ryker threatened, waving his spoon towards his roommate who had his back turned. *Not looking totally stops the threats happening, right?* That was usually Grayson's logic at least as he walked out of the room.

Ryker walked out of the kitchen with his own treats, following after Grayson. Of course Grayson had first dibs on seating and got comfortable, with his legs slung over the arm of the side chair he was sitting in. At least he left Ryker with the couch to sit on, and he found it more comfortable than the chair anyways. He even fell on it with a slight bounce.

"What's tonight's plan?" Ryker asked.

"There's this new movie someone told me about with a lot of dialogue and story telling music. I thought it would be fun," Grayson stuck his tongue out between his lips momentarily, thinking, before speaking again. "And it's already in so we might as well watch it."

Ryker picked up the TV remote and prepared himself to start searching for the movie Grayson wanted the moment he responded. "Okay, let's watch it."

~~

"You've been working a lot of late shifts recently." Grayson spoke walking into one of the two bedrooms and sat down on Ryker's bed. Hugging the first pillow in arms distance, he rocked slightly. He mostly kept his head turned towards Ryker's position or assumed position the entire time.

After the movie ended, Ryker had disappeared to his room to try and get some schedules planned for his work in peace. He tried sitting on the ground near his bed to get his work flow to activate in its own strange way—but obviously that wasn't going to end up working. Or at least it wasn't going to happen until Grayson decided to go to sleep. *Needy Grayson.*

"I didn't think you would notice that."

Grayson rolled his eyes, leaning forward where he

sat to be closer to his friend sitting on the ground. Ryker leaned back on his hands as he looked up with a frown.

"It's strange and I think you know that." Grayson commented. "All your late nights going out for work, it doesn't make sense. It makes me feel like that roommate in comic books that doesn't know their roommate is a good or bad guy in the city."

"Look, I can explain, okay? Recently I've been—" Ryker started to compile the lies he has told before. Spinning the mental wheel of the one he would be telling that day. Visiting friends who really needed him, covering someone's shift at work, maybe sleepwalking? Sleepwalking would be a new one.

"Ryker!" Grayson exclaimed in the middle of Ryker's talking.

"Wh—" Ryker was met with a pillow straight to his face, cutting off his sentence.

A laugh echoed in the room as he lifted his head to look at his friend. His normal childish smile was present, his hands on his feet the whole time he swayed side to side, "Ha! I got you! I tricked you!"

Ryker took a deep breath, regaining his composure and picking up the pillow which had been used as ammunition before. Lifting his head up off the bed he leaned back against, not giving Grayson the satisfaction of guessing his expression. "Want to get it over with or should I give you a few seconds of a headstart to try and run?"

"Are you really going to threaten your blind friend? You were the one being mean! You know, by not hanging out with me and not giving me real reasons why?"

Ryker got to his feet, his hands tightened their grasp on the pillow in front of him and spun to face Grayson. He *gifted* Grayson another chance for picking. "Choice 1 or choice 2."

Ryker counted down in his head.

5…

4…

"How about neither?" Grayson asked, hopeful.

3…

"Pick." Ryker responded.

"Alix please don't." Grayson begged, his smile not faltering even faced with danger.

2…

Ryker didn't wait for one before launching the pillow at his friend. Grayson let out a wheezed laugh once the pillow hit. He fell back on to the bed, his arms wrapping around the weapons of attack. Self protection jumping in to stop Ryker from being able to grab the pillow and attack Grayson once more. Ammo taken just out of range.

"Truce?!" Grayson requested between laughs.

A war had begun but had he actually been ready to participate in it? This was something Grayson started, it had consequences and he had to deal with them.

Ryker walked towards his bed leaning over his friend who froze completely in his spot. His hand reaching up and over his friend, being placed in a position to keep him from completely falling down on him. Or was that what he was doing?

"Alix, truce?" Grayson asked.

Grayson smiled up trusting Ryker like he usually tended to. Not seeing the obvious traps even when they were laid out right in front of him and Ryker was ready to set them off.

Ryker leaned close to him, "Never," quickly pulling away and hitting his friend with the other pillow on the bed before he could expect it. A yelp escaped Grayson as he rolled out of the way of another attack.

The edge of the bed coming quicker than either of them expected. Ryker reached out to try and stop his friend from rolling off but it was too late, he was falling to the ground with a partial bang. Ryker took in a sharp breath as he looked at his unmoving friend.

"Grayson?" Ryker took a step towards his friend but got no response. His heart leaping in his chest, pounding against the cage it was trapped inside. "Grayson!"

Ryker knelt down next to his friend. His hand was placed just against the other's shoulder when Grayson quickly sat up and spun around. A pillow hit Ryker in the face causing him to fall back against the wooden ground.

"Sneak attack!" Grayson jumped to his feet, raising his hands up in victory while Ryker sat up again.

The standing boy danced with his self claimed victory without even checking to make sure the other was down. No trophy or even verbal confirmation even came, just his own thoughts of a win. In the end who exactly was going to tell him if he did or did not win? No one was going to stop him.

He cheered and spun, nothing being able to take his victorious smile from his face for he had won against

Ryker. Deception was necessary but the war was over.

Ryker slowly rose to his feet, his eyes on the boy in front of him. A sinister grin formed on his face. His arms lifted and turned slightly behind him as he readied the pillow in his hand "Oh you're so on."

It came harshly down, colliding with Grayson in an instant.

How are we even friends?

~~

"Sit here while we call your mom." A new first grade teacher led a small child towards a row of seats along the wall near the front office desk. She beamed at the little child and kept at it as he climbed into the chair. It was like she thought the more she smiled at him the more behaved he would become.

"She won't come."

"Why do you think that, Ryker?"

Ryker looked up into his teacher's golden hazel eyes, watching her brush her black licorice like hair behind her ears waiting for his response. He rubbed his thumbs together, tilting his head down towards them and breaking his gaze with the teachers.

*"She **has** to work." Ryker mumbled.*

The teacher just nodded, getting up to her feet and walked towards the secretary to speak with her. Ryker frowned, watching how the dark red and dried blood flaked off of his knuckles—floating to the ground.

"Wanna band aid?"

12

Ryker tilted his head to see another boy sitting a few seats down, copper hair shining with sun that beamed down on him. Bright colorful band aids covered his knees, visible as he kicked his feet back and forth. He smiled widely letting Ryker see he was missing one of his teeth. He was holding out what should have been a small white packaging but Ryker could see the bright orange bandage that came through.

"No." Ryker all but snapped.

The other boy laughed at the angered response. He got up from his seat and slid into the one beside Ryker. He held his hand out in an offering of a handshake, "My name is Grayson Merlin Finch. It's nice to meet you."

"That is a stupid name, bird." Ryker mumbled.

"Well mom always told me to be proud of it." Grayson responded. He shook his hand out where it sat, waiting. His tongue bit between his teeth as he waited patiently. "What's your name?"

Ryker stared down at his hand for a moment before allowing his to take position against Grayson's. "Ryker Alix Griffin."

"Nice to meet you Alix!" Grayson didn't flinch like people normally did as Ryker glared at him. "If we are going to be best friends we need nicknames."

"We aren't going to be best friends."

"Yeah we are."

~~

Less than half an hour later Ryker was the only

moving body in the room as he walked through the room with a blanket he had grabbed from another room in his hands. The slightly heavy weighted blanket sagged in his arms until he reached the end of the bed and threw it on to the end.

"How do you carry this thing with your other stuff everytime we go to your parent's house to stay the night? It's so heavy, Gray." Ryker asked with a slight whine. He knew why he had it but how did he carry this weight around?

He pulled the heavy blanket over the sleeping body, making sure to tuck the sides just a little bit before laying one of his own fuzzy blankets over the top. For just a moment he debated with himself on if it was good enough before he stepped back leaving Grayson alone to sleep.

Grayson was his best friend, but that made him a weakness. He was such a distraction and it was so obvious too.

"You're such an idiot." Ryker muttered starting on a quest for a plethora of items in his room. When he had what he wanted scooped into his arms he walked towards the door only to stop before completely leaving.

Ryker glanced back at his peacefully sleeping friend who had completely taken up his bed for his own wants and needs. A small smile formed on his face and he had to force himself to look away once again.

He flipped the light in the room off as he spoke. "Goodnight Gray. See you in the morning."

He closed the door with a quiet click before he walked towards the living room with his items in an uncomfortable hunched over hold. Maybe he will get some of his unofficial work done before he goes to bed—the schedule did have to go out by tomorrow afternoon though. It had to push it off when he decided to go out that night but he thought that he would be able to get back on track now.

But a yawn escaped from Ryker.

So maybe it was time for bed. Work had waited this long, it could definitely wait another day to be finished.

Chapter 2

Various papers lay scattered on wooden floorboards. Books wobbled under their own weight in their stacks against the back of the couch. Their home in the living room with no particular order to the stacks. The TV in the living room played the local news. Ryker sat between all the laid-out items, shuffling through them all in a decision on what was necessary and what was not at the current moment of time and planning. It was a tedious and not quite necessary task, yet he sat there to do it anyway. The chaos of it all never scared him, and he liked to see everything in its unassigned placement. Books with books, sales reports put together with scheduling and time off requests, and then research about recent attacks through the city were in their own pile.

There were many things that Ryker could say about his life but the best thing to say was that his life was just chaos. No sign of order in sight, just a complete messy chaos.

"You're such a mess."

"Oh, shut up Grayson, I've seen your room." Ryker scoffed.

Grayson's room was not as bad as he joked—especially not for someone with little vision—but it was funny to see the red emerging on Grayson's cheeks. The best part—in his own opinion—was that Ryker helped clean his room when Grayson was busy with his own stuff and asked for help, so if there was any mess it was likely Ryker's own fault. Could he really get mad at the person who drew elaborate designs in his carpet with the vacuum because of a small mess left behind? Probably, but Ryker refused to accept that answer.

Grayson tried to play it all off as he shrugged, walking with quiet steps through the living room he fell onto the couch with a bounce. "You can't mock the blind one for a dirty room, unless you try to tell me it's dirty.

Ryker rolled his eyes as he picked up one of the many papers to glance over the information that was listed on it. Some of the piles went to his actual work—a job he held at a local restaurant known as Myst Falls—and a lot of it connected to his night job.

The volume of the TV increased as Grayson most definitely messed with the controller that Ryker had left on the couch. If the news were left on some sort of device he could hear, he did not care what Grayson did with the TV. Grayson apparently had similar feelings because he ended up not turning the channel to one of his usual favorites, typically cooking competition shows or just plain creation shows.

"Whatcha doing?" Grayson peaked his head over the back of the couch as he spoke.

Ryker sighed, his flow would have been interrupted if it had been there in the first place. Luckily it had decided not to make an appearance. "Work."

"No du—"

"Breaking News. The downtown Ghost Tech building seems to have caught fire mere minutes ago. The cause is still unknown as firefighters work to clear the scene and evacuate everyone from the building."

Both men went silent as their heads turned towards the TV, big words in a red box appeared on the screen. Ryker stood up, his eyes widening, as the screen turned to a video of a burning building. The sound was off on the video, but you could see the people running from the building and no one could truly guess the sound that came from them. Some were maybe screaming, others letting out every curse in their vocabulary, and perhaps a few people weren't even saying or screaming bad things about the situation if it was even a bad situation for them. Ryker wondered what they were thinking to be so *calm?* Was that the right word?

The sound of a newscaster speaking rose from the mysterious silence again. **"Citizens evacuate in panic as the building is becoming increasingly more unstable."**

"What's happening?" Grayson asked. He heard the same exact words that Ryker did, but he likely didn't know if it was real or not. A random show that could be playing with a fake news segment. He needed confirmation on what was going on and the only person he trusted to give him a truthful answer was with him.

"Someone set a building on fire and everyone is freaking out," Ryker answered. He turned his head from the screen and towards his chaotic 'work' once again. All of it had been put off this long, it could wait a little bit longer. "I have to go to work."

"What? Alix, someone just set a building on fire! Are you crazy?"

Ryker shrugged, "Maybe a little bit."

He walked away from his spot and towards the front door of the apartment grabbing a black duffle bag that sat near the front door with an extra change of black cargo pants and a black bomber jacket on it. It was a bag he had placed there last night when preparing it. He was always ready for a sudden need for it and the items held inside. Besides it was easier to grab without question from Grayson.

"I'm a manager, someone has to go in even when part of the city is freaking out." Ryker said. "I'll be back soon Grayson, just stay safe,"

"Ryker—"

"I will be okay. I promise," Ryker stated. Grayson nodded, Ryker frowned as he glanced towards the front door rather than his friend or the TV anymore. This was a lie he was so used to telling his friend, it was becoming strangely natural to come out of his mouth. "I'll be back before seven, keep the door locked."

"See you then."

"See you later Gray."

~~

"I'm closing tonight Grayson so I won't be home until late." Ryker pulled his keys of the rickety overused holder they had been using for keys, coats, and even at some points when he had decided he was done with it Grayson hung up his cane. At least he was using it. Ryker had to watch him stumble and almost fall—he would have fallen if Ryker didn't catch him—on multiple occasions purely because he didn't want to use it. Maybe there was something else behind it but Ryker couldn't read minds.

"Grayson?"

The apartment was unusually silent and he was earning no response from the one he called out too.

He put his keys back on the hook and walked back into the depths of the apartment. The living room was already cleared so Ryker decided Grayson's bedroom was a good place to look for the silent boy. He hadn't gone out that night had he?

"Gray?" The door was wide open, so Ryker took the first step in and found Grayson sleeping. He was okay. It was so early to be asleep yet such a routine for Ryker to leave at this time. He could admit he had fallen into this schedule himself leaving Grayson alone and by himself in this apartment with not much of an explanation other than work. That wasn't reasonable anymore. How was Grayson feeling after all this time?

Ryker turned his back to the room. "There is so

much I wish I could tell you, Gray. But it would just be putting you into danger if I told you the truth."

Walking out and unaware of the lifted hand and faint, "Huh?"

~~

Addresses were easy to find despite the midst of panic. Police scanners were going crazy, social media was being updated in an undiscussed rotation, and the easiest path was just following those running away from the chaos. Apparently there was no distance far enough for them to calm down by, Swerving and weaving in and out of running people was exhausting.

Ryker shoved his way against the lines of people running in groups away from something that happened to be going on. He had to park his car a few blocks down when the streets got jammed up by civilians, from there he had to risk the walk in the hysteric crowd and smoke. The smell of smoke hit him harder than he had expected it to. His hand shot up to cover his mouth to stop his gag from becoming something more than that. It was not the time for those reactions.

Another's body collided with his own knocking him back with a stumble. His hand grabbed their arm as they spun towards him and yelled a simple word.

"Run!"

Ryker let go of them and they ran past before he continued on his path instead of turning and following him and the rest of the group. With his free hand, he grabbed a piece of fabric from his pocket—a lone black mask. He risked pulling it over the bottom half of his face in public leaving just his dark jade green eyes left revealed. His mahogany brown hair waved close to covering his eyes but not enough to block his vision completely. Even though there were risks he doubted anyone would have paid more attention to him then the situation around.

"No one should be on floor 20, but that's where the fire started and it has been cleared already."

It should have been harder than it was but Ryker easily listened to a conversation between two police officers who had been stationed out on the streets. While those two stood there others attempted to handle the panic of citizens and calm the situation. But even when they did attempt they just ended up standing there while firefighters were working to clear the building and put the fire out.

The building was almost surrounded though and taken over by law enforcement whose job was to keep out civilians who may want to play hero now or later on. But that did not mean it was impossible for someone to get inside.

~~

When a building is claimed to have 20 stories why might there only be 19 labeled in the elevator? Of course it would make sense if it was not talked about but it was spoken about like more accessible areas to the public like the parking garage and commercial floors. It didn't seem to exist, yet how were there key cards labeled with access to it and every other door in the building.

Ryker should not have been able to access any of the many floors that he had walked onto, yet there he walked through the halls anyway. It hadn't been too hard to swipe the keycard off of a panicking civilian when he needed it. When he was done with it he could easily leave it lying in the building, giving that civilian the much—needed excuse of losing it in the attempts to run. No one had to get in trouble that way. Ryker preferred when no one had to get into any trouble, it was better that way.

He walked carefully up a back staircase he had located that had not been overrun with panicking civilians and firefighters who were attempting to do their jobs. Passing them would be a lot harder than finding this second path which led him up to the location he wished to get to. The empty halls of the office building. He wasn't even sure people knew about the staircases' existence though. Being in the back of the building exiting into a dark alley didn't make it the most convenient for escaping and being tucked in a back hallway just worsened the ability to find it. Whoever built the building didn't think this through, but luckily for the employees it seemed like the ones making fire safety plans did.

"19?" Ryker stopped in front of the door that was sitting at the top of the winding staircase he just ascended. A frown formed as he looked at the locked door. He did not know what was stranger, the lack of a floor 20 or the lack of smoke the entire way up the staircase. It should be filled with smoke at this point unless somewhere closer to the fire there was a hole taking the smoke out.

"This isn't right."

Ryker bit the inside of his cheek as he went and swiped the keycard. A beep preceded a click as the door unlocked for him. Pushing the door open he revealed the long seemingly endless hallway that lay out in front of him.

"Oh goodie." Ryker mumbled in a higher voice than he normally spoke. He knew he had a horrible habit of talking while working but sometimes it just came out.

The long walk down the hall began. Ryker started his search for something out of place along the boring uniformed hallway, each room he checked looked the exact same with a used desk, a dull beige filing cabinet, and gray-blue carpets. Maybe he was looking for something that was not there to begin with—something nonexistent.

"Help!" A yell echoed through the hallway.

While that had not been what he was looking for Ryker began to run in the direction of the voice that continued to cry out for help. He pushed open each door in hopes of reaching the person as their voice grew louder and louder with each step he took. All until he finally located a wide-open door.

"Please!" A woman cried out.

Ryker stepped into the room, his eyes instantly being pulled to look at the support beam that had fallen from the roof, with the damage of the fire, and now lay on one of the woman's legs. Her eyes grew in shock the moment that Ryker stepped into what definitely wasn't an office room.

"Please help me!" She begged as Ryker ran forward, he knew he could not lift it alone but perhaps he did not need to.

"I'm going to need your help to do this," Ryker spotted some thick metal piping that sat laying on the ground nearby the woman. It was broken off from its intended location but he was sure he could get it to work how he needed it to. So he grabbed it and started to wiggle it under the beam. "When I tell you, I need you to try and lift the beam up. Okay? Can you do that?"

The woman nodded. Ryker took a deep breath as he shoved the pole to get under the beam, wiggling it an extra bit to make sure it was under just enough that he believed his plan would work.

"Okay on three." Ryker said before he started his count. "1. 2. 3!"

Ryker applied pressure down on his end of the pole as the woman tried to push the support beam up. He listened to the creak of the pole under pressure when it began to bend at the end near the beam. He leaned down on the object, adding as much of his weight as he could against it as he tried to lift the beam before the pole could snap.

"Come on," Ryker muttered.

A gasp escaped the woman, his head snapped in that direction to see the beam very slowly lifting. Her foot wiggled as she tried to pull it out from under its original trapped position. The second her foot was free, the pole snapped, and the beam came crashing back down against the ground. Ryker fell forward to the ground with nothing more to lean on.

"Thank you!" The woman gasped out.

Ryker carefully pushed himself to his feet, wiping

dirt and dust from the floor off of his clothes. His nose wrinkled at the sight of the brown and gray on his hands.

Disgusting Ryker thought before turning his head towards the woman. Her legs seemed unburnt but still were scratched up. He watched for a moment until he saw her beginning to wiggle her feet. Then he spoke, "Where's floor 20?"

"Wha—"

"Floor 20. People might be trapped up there. How do I get to it?" Ryker asked harshly as he picked up his broken pole again examining it for use. It was frail, unlikely to last him in any sort of fight like he wished for it to. It was in better use laying there on the ground as a decoration then anything else at this point. The fire had ruined it.

The woman looked around, biting her lips as she looked everywhere but where Ryker happened to be standing still. His patience grew thin without an answer. Perhaps it was lucky for all of them that the woman decided to answer though.

"Down this hall there is another staircase. Please do not tell anyone I told you."

"You shouldn't worry so much about other people right now."

Ryker finally took a chance to glance around the room he had entered to help the woman when he heard her cries. It wasn't actually a room like he had suspected but instead a short hallway with another door at the end of the hallway. Red **Do not enter** words sprawled across the door but were not barring entrance into the area that the door led to. Smoke creeped out from the cracks above and below the door.

"Fire and rescue are downstairs, go find them a few floors down and they will get you out of here." Ryker spoke as he started to walk towards the red words. "You never saw me here."

"What are you going to do?" The woman asked.

"I'm going to save everyone."

~~

Up a thin ascending staircase smoke grew heavier and heavier. The closer he got to a cracked open door the glacial silence became abnormally apparent. A static sat nestled in his ears until it clicked in his mind that it was not static as expected but rather a crackling of fire. The whirling of a going sprinkler suppressed by the fire's noise.

The door was warm, and with a kick it swung in revealing the full damage of the hidden floor in front of Ryker. Fire surged through the floor and covered the walls and ceilings surrounding the mainly open area. It was only where the fire had gotten too bad that Ryker had not been able to see past and get a good idea of what was there and more than likely getting turned to ash. Heat radiated to even the wet area where he stood. Strangely it seemed to be the only exit other than a large hole that was created in the brick wall by something. An explosion?

"Hello? Is anyone still up here?" Ryker called out in worry of trapped workers as he moved into the way of the spraying water. A sizzle escaped from the floorboards beneath his feet with every creaky step he took.

"You shouldn't be up here."

Looking in the direction of the voice, Ryker spotted a person moving from the shadows and into clear view. The fire shining light on his hidden away face. The gas mask they wore hid just about any signifying features of the man there—just like the black full bodysuit they wore worked to hide the rest of their skin—but it didn't stop the twinge of recognition that stung in Ryker's mind. Why were they here? Who were they?

"You set the fire." Ryker stated.

"Everything bad has to go." The masked man spoke.

Ryker yelled. "How stupid are you? You're killing people!"

The masked man took slow steps towards Ryker who stood in what he believed to be the only way out. To get out they would have to go through him, and he did not plan to make it so easy if he wasn't going down to a police car. If he was going down for something they better have two police cars ready because this dude was going to come down with him.

"*They* wanted this. I have to follow orders, maybe you should learn to as well and stop messing up our plans," The masked individual spoke with a tired sigh. "This is your only and last chance to get in line. They don't like people who get in the way of the mission. I will not be allowed to be so nice next time we meet."

Ryker gritted his teeth, taking a step forward and causing the floor to let out a loud creak beneath him.

"Don't worry there won't have to be a next time."

"And what are you going to do?" The masked man asked. "I know who you are, you cannot do anything legally. Logically, within the next 2 to 5 minutes you shall be passed or dying from smoke inhalation without a suitable mask to help you. Is that what you wish for?"

"No, but I do know something that I can do legally." The floor shook beneath Ryker's feet—like his morals shook in his brain with more illegal possibilities—as he took a single step towards the masked man. His eyes scanned over the small room as he looked for any potential ways out. "I'm making a citizen's arre—"

His final words never finished as the floor made a final loud creak.

Chapter 3

"You said you would be okay."

Ryker frowned from their couch, an ice pack held to the side of his face by his friend sitting there with the ice pack in hand. He was working on bandaging his other injuries with his friend's help in the other field. It generated some struggle to work that way but Grayson had begged to be able to help and Ryker couldn't deny him.

"I know Grayson, I didn't mean to get hurt," Ryker let out a sigh. "Everyone was just in a panic on the streets. I got shoved down and it was difficult to get up. I did my best to get out of the way and wait for things to calm down."

"You shouldn't have gone," Grayson responded. "The restaurant didn't need you."

Grayson just didn't understand why he had to go and Ryker knew that, but it wasn't that easy to explain. He hadn't told him anything about his secret nighttime habits up to this point and they had lived together for years. It was too late to be able to tell him now, right? Too many late nights with lies for explanations he would have to take back. How could he explain years of this kind of work to him? Grayson would never understand.

"How do I make it up to you?" Ryker asked.

"Alix, this isn't just some random mistake you make up for with movies and ice cream," Grayson exclaimed. He threw the ice pack in his hand down onto the couch, standing up he backed away from his friend. "You could have been seriously hurt and I would have had to answer that hospital phone call again! I can't deal with that!"

Ryker stood up. "You and I both know that was nothing. It was a minor concussion and they only called you because I needed a ride. Something you couldn't give me!"

His hands curled into shaking fists by his sides while he looked at the boy in front of him. A watery look dawned in Grayson's eyes. Sniffles escaped the previously yelling male, his head turning to look away from his best friend. His shoulders shook his eyes down at the ground unable to make the usual connection.

"If you keep doing stupid things I'm going to lose you, Ryker. I don't want to lose you *too*." Grayson said, his voice trembling with the words he said. He raised his hand, wiping away the tears forming in his eyes.

"Hey," Ryker walked towards Grayson. His legs ached with every step but he kept on towards his friend.

"I'm sorry, okay? I am going to keep myself safe, you are not going to lose me."

"Promise?"

"Yeah, I promise."

~~

The next morning Ryker made a simple promise to Grayson, he was going straight home after work. It happened to be the only way to get Grayson out of the car that morning. He had a job interview that morning, he should be holding an unnecessary ground today.The last place he worked had closed a few weeks ago and since then Ryker had been working as many extra and double shifts as he could just so they could pay their bills. He worked on the restaurant floor a lot more than he ever wished to.

"Did you hear about that building that almost burnt down?"

With the promise Ryker made, he actually had to go to work and listen to the gossip of his employees no matter how annoying they were. With everything that happened the night before it could be expected that this would be most of the gossip for the day. He was just going to have to listen and try to avoid caring about it.

"Yeah, I did. My whole family was watching the news for hours."

Ryker walked past the youngest worker, a 17-year-old, and another one of the employees who was assigned to work the opening shift. He didn't care much for the conversation, there was nothing they could say that would matter that much to him. As long as they were setting up tables and not bothering him as they worked he couldn't care less.

"My girlfriend was a firefighter on the scene." Or perhaps the older girl speaking could grab his attention for a moment. "Apparently they were told to stay off floor twenty, but no one knew who gave the command."

"Are you being serious, Sofi?" The teenage worker, Brooke, asked.

"Yeah, I'm serious," Sofi responded. Ryker turned his head towards the pair that had stopped walking and working. "They are trying to figure out who gave the order because that person is going to be in a lot of trouble and none of them want to be that person."

"That seems pretty bad. How can they not know who gave the order if they all listened?"

"How should I know? I wasn't there and working on the site. I would love to work as a firefighter though. I would get to see my girlfriend all the time."

"Shouldn't you two be working on your current job instead of daydreaming about Sofi's girlfriend?" Ryker finally raised his voice instead of keeping his thoughts to himself. This caused the jumping of his workers before they spun toward him. "Or are you planning on being in trouble like those firefighters?"

"No sir," Brooke said.

"Sorry, Ryke," Sofi muttered.

Ryker scoffed, turning towards one of their few cash registers, and began to open up for the morning. The two had walked off to hopefully continue their jobs but Ryker could still hear the whispers of their current conversation.

"Of course, he is grumpy today. The world could be burning and we would still be stuck with his attitude." Sofi muttered.

"Maybe something happened. He seems hurt." Brooke responded. Ryker pulled the edge of his sleeve to try and get it to cover any possible bruising from the fall. Bandages he wore bulked up his clothing already making it difficult to hide. The red scabbing marks down the right side of his face didn't help, nor did the way he put more weight on one leg then the other. But with the herds of people coming in that day would cause a rapid shift off of him.

"Nah, that's rarely it. I'll go buy him something caffeinated before we open, that should work to boost him up. Maybe it'll make him happy for at least a minute."

Ryker sighed. This was going to be a long day.

~~

Too many diners had put in requests for the news to be put on. After about the twelfth request Ryker snapped, switching the TV on to some of what he thought were the most boring sports he could find. Everyone just wanted to see any sort of update on the unexplained fire from the night before; they wanted to know the danger they were or weren't in without even knowing what had actually happened.

Terrorist attacks? A simple mistake from someone in the building? Or was it something else hidden from the building? Too many theories were thrown around without any evidence of any of them being accurate. The news wasn't even helping either—their own theories and stories spiraling through the brains of their watchers. Someday they would learn they didn't need to have the next big scoop.

"Ryker, we got another request for the news." Marc, one of the few hosts on the clock, said as he leaned against the bar counter Ryker stood behind. Usually Marc preferred a position behind the bar but today he was needed on the floor as a host to cover the chaos.

"Seriously?" Ryker let out a sigh, picking up the remote he looked up at the multitude of TVs and started to look through different channels the restaurant owned. "What sport shall we be watching now Marc? Golf is on. Or maybe cricket."

"What's cricket?" Marc asked.

Ryker shrugged. "Heck if I know, might as well make everyone mad though. Maybe they will finally learn that we can't play the news here though and they will stop asking."

"Yeah about that. Why can't we play the news?"

"I don't know," Ryker answered. He walked out from behind the bar as the bartender he was covering arrived back from their break. "I just know the people who bought the company hate the news being broadcasted. You were given the same orientation I was."

Ryker walked towards the back of the restaurant to check on the kitchen staff before he had to clock out for the day. Marc glanced behind him towards the host stand to make sure his coworkers were okay before he trailed after his boss.

"Yeah that's because they are always on it," Marc said. "And nowadays it's almost never in a good way."

Ryker turned, sending the employee a warning glance before nodding his head towards a black circular camera that sat hidden in the top corner shadow above them. Hidden from sight where only a few knew where to find them.

Ryker forced a smile onto his face before looking back at his employee. "If you have any complaints you can take them up with my boss. I can contact them for you if you want. Otherwise, I believe it's wise for you to choose your next words carefully."

"No complaints here." Marc smiled, throwing his hands up while he spoke. "I'll be going back to work now. See you later Ryker."

"Bye Marc."

Ryker turned back around and headed towards the break room. He was done with dealing with the customers and even his own employees who seemed to lack the ability to tell customers no and their policy. His shift was due to be over any minute now. It was time for him to go home.

~~

First days were supposed to be filled with excitement not dread which buried itself in the pits of the stomach, begging and clawing to get out and show the world. First days were full of sweaty hands being wiped on thrifted dress pants. A teenage boy shouldn't be this nervous about his first day of work, well that wasn't true with the natural feeling. But he really shouldn't be this nervous about talking with the beaming woman waiting for him the moment he entered the restaurant.

A bright smile staring at him, burgundy lips intense compared to the black dress that stretched down to her knees. Her hair was tugged and spun into a messy bun, the skin at the root of her hair pulled back as well. Two clipboards held against her chest, freshly painted apple red nails tapped against the glossed over thin wood. Impatient waiting but her smile never faltered.

"Hello Mr. Griffin!" A silky gloved hand hovered for the new employee. His hands were sweaty though, he couldn't ruin those perfect gloves. She lowered her hand after a few minutes. "Our other hire is waiting for us. Let's begin your orientation."

The woman spun on her flawless black heels, despite being a walking and dirty environment he was pretty sure there wasn't a single spot on them. Speaking of, he was also confident in the fact that her whole outfit was spotless.

"I'm going to keep this brief, my name is Charlotte Sallow but you will refer to me as Mrs. Sallow. Dana operates everything here, if you have a question or problem you will go to her." Mrs. Sallow started her ramble the moment they had met with the other new hire. "We have very few rules but one we are strict on is no news."

"No news?"

"Correct Mr. Laurier. We don't associate with

fabulists." Mrs. Sallow continued. "Which means no speaking with them, letting their channels play, or even step foot inside."

"Why not?" Mr. Laurier asked.

Charlotte glanced over at her two new employees, "Because they don't tell the truth. They craft lies, spinning their webs around all those foolish enough to listen. We don't associate with them and neither will you."

She rambled so much about the news that Ryker knew his eyes had left her to scan the restaurant of people this was happening in front of. It wasn't too full of a building at this time but a few of the tables were taken up. An older couple in the far back right, someone waiting for a date near the front, and then two people sitting in a booth nearby. A pairing that seemed sibling like as the alot older one—back towards Ryker—read a book while the younger tried to steal and eat his fries.

Mrs. Sallow stopped in her tracks, once again she held her hand out to the employees for a shake. "Do we have an understanding?"

Mr. Laurier grinned at the offer of a shake, taking Mrs. Sallow's hand, finishing the binding contractual action. He was hers.

Mrs. Sallow shifted her hand in Ryker's direction once more. He stared down at it for a moment knowing exactly what it would mean if he did or didn't shake it. His entire future relying on one action and the words to back it up. He wasn't aware of a single person who wouldn't shake her hand.

But he shook his head no.

"What?"

"Sorry, germaphobe." Ryker shrugged with his lie.

"Oh, you will do so great in this line of business." Mr. Laurier scoffed but Mrs. Sallow couldn't take her eyes off him.

Yes he would be.

~~

"I'm clocking out," Ryker said, walking swiftly through the employee break room. His shift was over and he wanted to get out of this place as soon as possible—just like every employee here. Hanging up his black apron and clocking out on the computer, he was now ready to leave.

"Bye Ryke!" Sofi, who was on break, leaned back in her chair to speak with the leaving manager. "Say hi to that roommate of yours for me!"

"You know I won't, and don't call me that." Ryker closed the break room door with a slam, leaving behind a laughing Sofi. They both were well aware of what would and would not be done. Work and home life were always to be kept separate, except in a few cases and Sofi had somehow figured out exactly how to become one of those cases.

I'm never letting Grayson throw another party. Ryker thought.

One Halloween party, Grayson had invited over both of their coworkers and now people knew stuff about his life and he was not pleased with that for sure. Little bits of information she learned came out at random and surprised Ryker when they did. There was so much stuff he didn't even know how she figured it out within the few hours she was at the apartment.

"Hey, Ryker!"

As he walked through the restaurant a few people gave small waves or called out hellos and goodbyes to the worker. He responded with a simple combination of a smile and a nod. He did happen to stop at one of the tables to talk with a group of regulars before making his planned exit so he could go home.

On the way out Ryker pulled his phone out only to be instantly greeted by the explosion of notifications from news sites he followed. Many of them talking about the events from the night before but not in a way he expected.

Missing Fire?

What's the government hiding?

Videos of last night's fire are gone!

"What?" Ryker muttered to himself at the sight of the news.

Skipping the first two and opening the third of the article options he could see more in-depth what was going on. Rumored was that all videos from the events of the night before on the internet were gone. Big news channels had taken down their uploaded videos, civilian-posted videos were getting banned and taken down, and nothing and no one was explaining why it was happening or even what was happening.

Why were those videos being taken down? It didn't make sense. Things like this get posted all the time, so what was different about this time?

There was something on those videos that someone didn't want to be seen. Perhaps he needed to get a hold of a copy of a video of the building being on fire. But where could he get a copy of a tape of the building?

Ryker slipped his phone into his pocket. His fingers hit a thin square plastic item that he had shoved into his pockets that morning during his rush to get out of the apartment with Grayson. A curious hum escaped him as he wrapped his fingers around the item and pulled it out to look at what sat in his hand now.

A stolen work ID that did not match the government ID in Ryker's wallet which still sat in his pocket from this morning. A grin formed on the man's face as he looked at the key card to the doors of a certain building. A key card he meant to drop to a place where it would be found on its own in the future but he must have forgotten when he fell.

"Seems that you are going to be useful once again."

Chapter 4

Calm was unusual. Nothing was ever calm so when the drive from work to the office building was a calm smooth ride Ryker knew something was off. Many people in the city were either still at work or had gone home just a few hours prior leaving the perfect gap to make it through the city without much difficulty. That didn't mean it was completely clear on the street but it didn't mean traffic was crazy either.

Ryker parked in a parking lot two blocks from his desired location—an office building cleared the day prior. He changed into a white shirt and his black bomber jacket as well as some black pants before ditching his car for the rest of the journey. He did wait to be a few minutes away from his car before pulling his mask on. Anything that could be used to figure out his identity wasn't good, so it was best to put distance between him and it—even if the walk was painful. Security in keeping his identity secret was worth all the trouble.

The building happened to be less surrounded with law enforcement, firefighters, and civilians now then it was the previous night but there is logic to explain that. *Who goes back to their office the day after a building gets caught on fire? Who would want to cause a company-wide panic where people almost died*? What law enforcement group would allow people back into a burning building without monitoring and checking around for a source?

With that thought, why was there a car parked in the office's parking lot?

There were no blue or white colors on the car like the city's official police cars held on top. There were no red, blue, and white lights on the top. There wasn't even what seemed to be a police license plate. So if it wasn't a police car when whose car was it and what did they want with this place?

This isn't right. Ryker thought to himself as he walked leisurely down the sidewalk and towards the office he had gone to the night before.

Or maybe he was just paranoid. A public parking spot taken up by a civilian who found it easier to park and walk than wait for an empty spot at their deserved location to open up. An obvious solution to a rapidly forming problem.

Even if he was just a little bit paranoid his hands sat in his pocket, one wrapped around the key card and the other around a folded metal blade he kept in the glove box of his car almost all the time after one of his first missions like this. He learned an important lesson during that time.

"Just a few drug dealers, I can handle that. It's going to be so easy."

It wasn't as easy as he thought as a sixteen year old who decided to face three men much bigger than him. He didn't have so much as a knife or any sort of fighting and self defense classes being taken prior to defend himself.. He never said he was smart and a lot of things had changed from then. He learned his lesson the moment his mom had to pick him up from the hospital with a broken arm and a concussion—it was probably one of the last of his missions his mom got to witness the aftermath of and get a say put in about how it went down. No way he was going to make the same mistakes.

Now it was better to be prepared than dead.

Police should be surrounding this place in the search for evidence to what happened and to keep any possible evidence safe. If something like the video footage went missing after a fire then the news would cause an issue. So the police had to be here to protect it. Unless they were given the order to not be there. None of this made sense. What was going on?

I wonder of Sofi's girlfriend had been given any orders like this recently.

He was never going to ask her or Sofi for confirmation though. Just imagining their suspicions on what he was doing was enough to deter that wave of thought before it could crash into existence.

Ryker walked up to the building, swiping the stolen keycard to hear, listening to the beep of the door which swung open to let him in. The first floor smelt of the reminisce of smoke from the night before. White walls and tiled floor stained with soot and ash that had gotten to this floor. Footsteps left on the floor from the chaos and those trying to do their jobs the previous night.

Ryker wiped his fingers against the wall, gray coming off earning a scrunched up disgusted look from him. Okay, he wasn't a germaphobe in any way but the walls were revolting. He just wanted to stop and scrub them until they were clean again.

Why did I do that? Scoffing at his own actions Ryker attempted to wipe the ash off just leaving gray streaks on his black pants instead. But he couldn't focus too much on that, he had other things he needed to be doing.

"Okay, if I was a surveillance room where would I be?" Ryker asked himself. Ryker looked down at the ground and spotted the newest set of footprints on the ground. "I would be wherever the newest footprints are. Good job me."

Ryker gave himself a little pat on the back before he started to follow a set of well defined footprints; well one was easy to make out and the other happened to have a slight slide with each step. Perhaps a limp?

An intriguing detail which flowed through the river of thought into the back of his mind as he continued his journey deeper into the office building. Searching for the surveillance room alone was a hopeless journey but hopefully the footsteps were a well enough guide. Just in case, he did happen to look at doors as he passed them in hopes to find the wanted room. Of course each door he passed with no luck was just narrowing it down to the footsteps being right. The only problem—there was no set of leaving tracks.

Soon he was closing in on the last door of the hall and with nowhere else to go he had to make a choice: Continue following the footprints or Leave.

Ryker picked the former.

If he was going to do something stupid he was at least going to pick the option that might lead him to where he wanted to go instead of the one losing him everything. To death he happened to go then.

Ryker thought about pulling his mask off once he was alone—easily able to get rid of a few minutes of footage if needed—but quickly slipped it over his mouth and nose as he spotted an open door at the end of the hallway with a light coming out into the hallway. Someone was definitely here right now and despite wearing a mask he couldn't risk them hearing him in any way at all.

But why was someone here?

If someone was here they were likely the one erasing all the camera footage, right? That meant Ryker had to stop him before he could do that here.

Bending his knees and squatting down Ryker began to move towards the door, slipping his weapon from his pocket. His hand turned a ghostly white as he gripped the cold metal.

"Dang it!" Ryker stopped moving at the exclamation of a somewhat familiar voice. But where did he recognize it from? "Come on you stupid machine!"

Ryker turned the corner, standing up straight once

again, his eyes landing on a person standing by the security computer typing away. A thumb drive flashed in the side of the middle computer in the room, probably put there by the other. And Ryker wasn't sure what was more recognizable about them; their full black bodysuit that they wore or their voice as they spoke angry words to the computer.

"Not a technology genius, huh?." Ryker crossed his arms, allowing himself to tilt slightly and lean against the doorway. The uncomfortable position he put his arm in was satisfying enough to see the other jump and spin towards him. Their hand moved to their side where something sat holstered. Ryker lifted his hand and gave a small finger only wave. "Nice to see you *again*."

"You shouldn't be here." They spoke. "I warned you I couldn't be nice this time."

"Of course you can't." Ryker responded. He took a test step forward, his eyes laid trained on the other's hand as they began to raise their weapon from the holster. He smiled at the sight, the other's only play having been revealed to him already.

Ryker reached his hand out, offering out a small shake of the hand. Shifting forward on his feet. "Maybe we should do some proper introductions. I can begin if it makes you feel better about it."

"Stay where you are and stop talking."

"How did I not recognize you before? How could I be so oblivious?" Ryker asked as he continued to walk towards the other and ignoring every order he was just given—he didn't care about someone else trying to order him around. With a flick of his wrist the blade of the knife in his hand opened to cold metal against his skin. "Deleting evidence looks pretty bad on you and your family, Alexander Sallow."

"Wh—"

Flicking his arm out, Ryker released the weapon in his hand to let it fly towards the other man in the room. A curse escaped Alexander as the weapon went past his hand, the blade moving across his skin.

"Now come on, don't bring a gun to a knife fight." Ryker joked.

Alexander revealed his bleeding hand, looking down at it for a moment before looking up at Ryker again. He snarled at his attacker. "You shouldn't have done that."

"Sorry but I can't let you go around deleting evidence."

"You don't understand why I have to." Alexander responded.

Ryker shrugged, "You have a choice, come with me to the police or-"

Alexander swung his fist hitting Ryker's face. Ryker stumbled back, hands shooting up to cup his nose with throbbing pain, warm liquid dripped between his fingers. The blood dripped down onto his white jacket. Alexander leaned forward as he spoke. "I pick choice two."

Ryker swung his right elbow up towards the other man, hitting him back to put space between the two of them. He grinned standing up and moving his hands down to his side with teary eyes.

"Violence," Ryker spoke with a laugh. His eyes laid on the man whose arms crossed over his stomach. "I can handle that."

Ryker struck again, not letting Alexander have a moment to regain his composure enough to grab the weapon he had waiting by his side. He shifted forward on his feet, his hand shooting out to try and grab the gun himself but something grabbed his hand. He traced the owner of the hand on his to the person in front of him—Alexander.

"That's not yours." Alexander spoke.

Ryker let out a gasp, doubling over as something hit into his stomach. Alexander smiled, taking a few steps forward as Ryker stumbled back with his arms crossed over his stomach.

"You never learn what your place is, do you? Now I have to take care of you once and for all." Alexander reached towards his side for his weapon.

Ryker straightened up, keeping his left arm crossed over his stomach as he lifted his right one with the item that now laid in it. "Looking for something?"

Ryker hovered his fingers over the trigger of the unfamiliar gun he had taken. His hand shook as he raised the weapon.

"Give that back." Alexander commanded. He took a half step back only moving his right foot back.

"I really don't want to have to do this. If you just put your hands up and no one has to get hurt." Ryker took his own very small steps forward as he spoke to Alexander. Alexander frowned at the comment before he slowly began to raise his hands into the air.

Everything about this situation screamed that it was

too easy to Ryker but sometimes that was just how things happened. There were plenty of ways to explain everything going on. The easiest—some people went down easier than others and those people just disappeared from the history books.

And other people didn't give up fighting.

Alexander's body turned as his leg rose and moved forwards the only other one in the room. Ryker couldn't think about the actions until the force was already made against his body and he was stumbling to the side.

Bang!

The noise echoed in his ears, a staticed ringing flooded over mere seconds later so Ryker couldn't hear the words that came from the others mouth. He did see Alexander turn away from him, his hand wrapped tightly around his upper arm. He also spotted smoke coming from the wooden wall where the bullet dug itself into a home.

Ryker let out what he expected to be a loud cough to clear the small breaths of smoke he was taking in. Pain shot through his chest with the simple action. He stumbled back and away from the other man who had his back turned as he attempted to regain his own composure. With his arm crossed over his stomach—the other being used to keep him up against the wall—he walked towards the door with a single wish, getting out of there. His body ached with every step he took.

He needed to get out of here.

Ryker turned, and his eyes landed on a thumb drive sticking out from the side of the computer. In lime green words the computer listened off the completion of the download of whatever was being taken from it. There wasn't much thought needed after the sight for Ryker to reach out, grabbing the drive from the computer and running towards the door. Running for an escape.

~~

Every single part of his body ached through the struggle to reach his car. What probably made the task worse was the sun which set behind him, and fast. Without the light of the sun it was left to the hanging lamps to light up the holes in the sidewalk, a job they couldn't do as they sat there broken. No one ever cared to come by and fix them even with numerous complaints from citizens.

The streets were even worse of a way to travel was just walking in the road. Stupid drivers, uncaring for the city laws, drove in their black cars at high speeds. Not a single light there to warn their presence to walking pedestrians.

I need to come here and fix some things Ryker thought. But he would have to wait a while before he could do some literal damage control in this part of the city. In the end it would be worth it though.

After too many chances to face death Ryker made his way to a crosswalk that would lead him to the recognizable parking lot. His car was the only one left on this side of the almost empty lot. A clear shot from here to there. And with the little white light man telling him it was safe to move across the street, he did so and walked quickly towards the safety of his vehicle.

The walk wasn't much further and he climbed into the complete safety of the vehicle. A gasp escaped the man as he fell into the seat, swinging his legs into the vehicle and closing the door with a loud slamming. He listened to the locks of the doors click before sinking into the car seat. He was missing his knife so he had to be careful not to linger in this area too long.

An exhausted sigh escaped from Ryker as he turned the car on, the lights flashing on above him allowing him to see part of the extent of his injuries. He shrugged off his jacket first before moving to pull up his shirt spotting the ugly forming pink and red bruising skin that lay underneath. His hand twitched up as he moved and touched the injury. The sound of a sharp intake of breath filled the silent car.

He was bleeding from somewhere yet he didn't know where and he didn't care too much about it. It wasn't a horrible amount and he could definitely survive it. Eventually he could have to take care of it though.

Control, rinse, dry, cover. Ryker thought to himself. The phrase his mom had taught him after about so many times of him coming home hurt from events he didn't even try to explain to her.

~~

"Are you ever going to tell me the truth or should I just keep waiting for the police to call one day when you are behind bars?"

There was only so much a mother could do,

especially when her son was determined to get himself killed by running off and doing something stupid without telling her about it until it was too late. She noticed her son's reckless abandonment when it came to his own safety since his friend's accident. Even if she wasn't able to be there all the time she knew something was going on.

"There is nothing happening. I promise." Ryker responded.

A sharp gasp escaped the teenage boy as a wet cold washcloth was dabbed against a nasty cut on the side of his face. It had been such a stupid thing for him to have gotten involved in and earned the injury. A fight had broken out in front of a store he just so happened to be walking by, too many people were becoming collateral damage for him to just keep on walking by.

"Ryker, I know when you are lying to me. I am your mother, we have this kind of magical ability."

"I stopped believing in magic when I was like ten, mom." Ryker scoffed only to pull away at the washcloth attacking once more. It burned every time his mom tried to press it against his face and it wasn't pleasant at all.

"Yeah but this is different from normal magic." His mom promised. "This is mom magic and we have this ability to tell when something is wrong with our kids whenever we talk to them. That is how I know something is going on."

"Mo—"

"I won't be mad, you can tell me."

Ryker's head fell forward, his gaze on the ground and away from the one member of his family left. The member of his family he had been lying to despite how many times they patched him up without question and how many lies they created when they were both out of the house and got questioned about his appearance.. Fights at school and sports were always some of her top picks.

"I want people to stop getting hurt. I've been wanting to stop their pain as long as I can. So I've started to do that exact thing. Stopping it all."

~~

Ryker's shaky hand reached out to the console in the middle of the dash, barely pressing the on button to allow the blaring radio to take up the car. A distraction from the pain that was going through him and the pain he knew would soon be coming with it. He had felt worse recently but just adding on wasn't something he was ready for. His whole body was going to be in so much pain.

"Oh crap." Ryker muttered, dropping his shirt down. He let his head fall back against the headrest. Black spots danced in his vision, blaring music filled his ears even though he remembered last putting the volume around 4 or 6. Never did he let it fall on to something that wasn't an even number. But his mind was too filled with dreadful thoughts to keep thinking of that. Instead it thought of what was to follow this event but really only one thing really seemed important at the time.

"Grayson's so going to kill me."

Chapter 5

Ryker didn't tell Grayson what had happened. He actually just called in sick for a week from work, coughing some and hiding out in his room with a 'headache', putting on an act sometimes in the apartment to keep Grayson out of the loop as well. He felt bad about lying to his best friend but he couldn't tell him. He made a promise, he wasn't going to let Grayson know he broke that promise. Sometimes lying was better than telling that sort of truth.

"Are you sure you are okay? You were sick for so long!"

Grayson worried too much but it just made Ryker worry that he made the wrong choice not telling him anything. He was freaking out but what was the point in making him? Three times within an hour he had asked the same question just because Ryker had began preparing to leave. He didn't deserve the panic. He didn't deserve the thousands of questions flowing down the river of thoughts in his mind, only a few slipping off his tongue for Ryker to answer.

In the end, it wasn't the questions that annoyed Ryker—even as he rolled his eyes and tried to get Grayson to stop talking—but rather the fact that he couldn't tell Grayson the truth. It would only worry and hurt him over something that had already happened and couldn't be changed. So Ryker decided to take his annoyance with himself and live with it, for Grayson.

"Last time you were sick you still went to work and refused to stay home. You just stayed off the floor so you wouldn't make customers sick." Grayson continued on. "If you were so sick you needed to stay home then—"

"I told you I am fine," Ryker promised, forcing out a weak cough. The forced cough hurting his throat more than his fake sickness. A burning tingle clawing up other coughs to clear the feelings now in his throat—the not real feeling."I just needed some rest and time off. You should know how easy it is to get sick working in my industry, there is no use getting my workers sick when we are just about to get to the busiest times of the year."

Grayson pouted in the passenger seat of the moving vehicle, he was bound to have walked off if they were in the apartment and not in the car. It was the hurtful and sad truth anytime Grayson felt like someone was lying to him, but some people needed space to figure out their thoughts.

"You can't be mad at me for nature taking its own course. Plus you are the one who wanted to go out and to the movie place for some reason." Ryker pointed out.

Grayson let out a questioning hum, slipping his red sunglasses on to his face, staring out the car window even if he wasn't actually watching the scenes going by at the time. Despite the sound of it Ryker knew it was actually accusing. Grayson was accusing him of being the reason they were at the bookstore and going out.

"Hey you wanted to come out too." Ryker finally said after a moment of silence between the two.

He took a right into the parking lot of the large old brick building that Grayson had requested they go to for their shopping destination that morning. Well less requested and more like a blanket hostage situation with going out to the bookstore and movie rentals being the items listed for the ransom. He just wanted to sleep and this is how he was being treated by the person who claimed to be his best friend. How rude?

"That's because the movie rental place is right next door." Grayson pointed out. Ryker rolled his eyes, quickly parking the car.

"Come on Gray, let's make this quick."

The two men exited the car. Ryker circled the car and jogged to Grayson's side, offering a hand out to him which was quickly smacked down. Grayson instead just pulled out his collapsible white cane that had mostly a red bottom, a white ball sitting at the end. It was his 'candy cane' stick, Grayson's words not Ryker's.

"Back off, Alix." Grayson snapped.

Ryker rolled his eyes, letting another cough escape him, a miniature smirk on his face that he tried to hide from anyone in view. "Whatever bird. Don't come whining to me when your fancy stick isn't helpful because you won't ever use it."

Grayson stuck his tongue out in a response, walking alone towards the sidewalk.

During his classes Ryker had learned that frequently the red meant the cane's user had low amounts of their vision left to use which did fit what was going on with Grayson's vision. It wasn't completely gone, but enough in which he could use the assistance if he wanted it— sometimes he dared not to with the hope of his feet gilding without trouble. Ryker was never a fan of that method, snatching up the cane on their way out in case Grayson wanted it. But it was only useful when the owner actually decided he wanted to use it and not keep it folded up on one of the many tables in the house.

It wasn't an object Grayson used constantly though so it rarely actually was a fact he remembered. Usually when Grayson got comfortable with a place it was used less and less, once more finding its lovely home waiting in the dust on a counter or table.A dusty imprint waited for it at home upon its return.

"You go find whatever book you were complaining about yesterday and I'm going to go rent some movies." Grayson scoffed.

He started walking left on the sidewalk like he knew to do. Typically that would be the right direction if Ryker had parked in front of the unbusy beauty salon like he usually did but today he did not do that. You can only park in the normal spot if there were actual spots available and not a line of cars snaking around the parking lot. Of course he probably should have told him ahead of time but Grayson hadn't given him the chance.

"Wait, Gray."

Ryker walked over to his friend pulling a red card from his pocket. He slipped the card into his friend's free hand. "First off, use my card. Secondly, the rental place is to the right. I parked in front of the bookstore today."

Grayson let out a dramatic gasp hitting his hand holding the card against his chest. "You changed it on me. Now I have to go rent all the expensive movies for this betrayal."

Ryker smiled, watching his friend slowly and carefully walk towards the rental building. He waited for Grayson to reach the tinted glass doors before he entered the large bookstore all alone. His eyes scanned over the many bookshelves that were sitting filled to the brim with books, people walking up and down the aisles between the different shelves in search for what they wanted or might want.

Luckily for everyone he already had his book wants in his mind so he wouldn't be wandering around in too much of an attempt to find something. Now he just had to find the correct section.

"Hello sir, can I help you find anything today?"

Ryker turned on his heel to face a woman wearing black dress pants and shirt, plus a dark green cardigan, who tried to speak to him. She had a pinned name tag on her cardigan reading *Rita* 'as well as an earpiece that was attached to a box clipped to her pants.

Ryker smiled at the woman, walking towards her.

"Yes, actually there is something."

~~

"How long does it take for you to pick out a movie?"

Ryker snapped his head to quickly glance at Grayson shuffling through the movies that he had rented for them to watch, before staring back at the road ahead. A large smile sat on Grayson's face as he ran his fingers over the DVD covers for what he had picked out. When Ryker had gone to get Grayson from the movie rental building he was in a deep grinning conversation with one of the workers there. Ryker hoped that meant Grayson liked the movies he picked out to listen to as he forced Ryker to watch the movie with him and describe the more intense scenes to him.

"It's a simple in and out thing." Ryker snapped his fingers. Such a simple concept.

"It's hard when you can't see what you are looking for," Grayson answered. "I have to get someone to tell me about them and the employee was busy. There was this giant line and I couldn't just pull them away to help me."

"Could have called me."

Grayson scoffed. The corners of Rykers mouth turned inwards and his eyes narrowed, eyebrows pulled close together. "Come on Gray, I would have answered if you had called me."

"Yeah sure Mr. My-Phone-Is-Never-Off-Of-Silent." Grayson mumbled. He held up one of the movies, his decision already made on what the first one being watched would be. His thumb ran over the cover with a small tactile on the top of it showing off the words and the design on top. A clear winner in his choice.

"Did you find what you were looking for?" Grayson asked.

Ryker glimpsed through the rearview mirror, his eyes landed on the small stack of books that sat in the back seat. "Yeah I found exactly what I was looking for, maybe even more."

"Good because I don't wanna come back here anytime soon if you are going to park in the wrong spot." Grayson huffed. He threw the DVD's in his lap and crossed his arms over his chest. "Like a jerk."

"I'm sorry, okay?"

"Traitor." Grayson mumbled. He slouched down in his seat, looking away from his friend in the driver's seat.

"Gray—"

"Traitor!"

Ryker scoffed. "Yeah next time I'll park in the already filled up parking lot. Great idea Gray, let's see how many tickets, arrests, and court cases I will be stuck dealing with afterwards."

They pulled into the parking lot in front of their apartment and Ryker parked the car. He turned towards Grayson but Grayson was already getting out of the car with his movies hugged against his chest. Ryker frowned at the sight of his friend walking away, but he didn't call out after him, instead reaching into the car to grab his books from the back, as well as a bag of items Grayson had gotten from who knows where. Grayson had only been in the movie rental building, there was no logical way for him to get something else.

Ryker shifted through his books until he reached the one he wanted and stopped moving the rest of them. He placed the most wanted on the top and closed the door with a loud slam, his eyes not leaving the item in hand. Grayson had disappeared into the apartment leaving Ryker alone in the car with the items he had bought that day.

An exasperated sigh escaped Ryker, he rubbed his fingers over the cover of the book where three people sat in what seemed to be a family portrait. Big white words sat at the top of the book cover.

The Sallow Family: A Full History

~~

Known for their business ventures in companies such as the Sallow Corporation and the restaurant chain Myst Falls, the Sallow family continues to grow and control much of the United States business. Also known for their many public appearances and international family popularity, Charlotte Sallow and Julian Sallow passed down their legacy in 2059 to their daughter.

On December 11th the Sallows' eldest child was born, guaranteeing the passing on of what would later be known as the Sallow legacy. By the age of 16 each Sallow child would be worth over millions of dollars. Earning their place in the Corporation their first daughter-

Page after page of useless information filled the books. With a few strange glances from the cashier and the excuse of needing them for research for his business major, he had gotten the books he was now deeming worthless. Over 30 dollars spent on books that were not even factually correct!

"For a family worth billions you would think they would make sure these books about them are correct. They don't even accurately talk about their actual first born chi—" Ryker stopped talking to himself for a moment. Grabbing one of the books he flipped to the table of context, his finger sliding down the page until he landed on one of the chapters.

Chapter 9 - The Year of Silence

Ryker turned to the beginning of chapter nine and read the first line out loud to himself. "After a year of silence from public view Charlotte Sallow, Julian Sallow, Alexander Sallow, and their newborn daughter, Olivia Sallow, made their appearance at the International Business Banquet."

Ryker scanned over the page with a smirk.

Seems they do accurately talk about your family. Guess this means it's time for me to do some research for my fake major after all, Ryker thought.

He leaned against the back of the couch, grabbing another book and skimming for a chapter labeled about a similar quiet year and he found it quicker than he expected. His smirk grew into a large grin, he settled back comfortably in the seat. Laying the book on his lap the research of the so popular Sallow family was able to begin.

Of course he only meant to spend a small amount of time today working on his small side project, but sometimes he did notice himself getting a little bit distracted.

"Alix, you have been in here for hours. Can I put one of my movies on?" Begged Grayson.

Perhaps that was something that he should work on.

"Yeah Gray, go for it."

He didn't bother to look up from the new book he had started, his pencil moving on the paper he had set up on his leg for his own personal notes. The couch cushions bounced with the new weight quickly on top of them. It's not like he was actually stopping the boy from watching his movies; Grayson had decided himself not to watch them until now.

Based on new known information following the dropped lawsuit against the Sallow corporation popular speculation has arisen with one important question that needs to be answered. Does the Sallow family have connections to the country's government?

If they do what does this mean for us as a nation—

"Having fun with your new books?" Grayson turned his head towards his roommate—and best friend—who had still been reading the book he had in his hands.

Ryker shrugged. "Highly informative."

"Oh really? That's good." Grayson said. He shuffled closer to Ryker, leaning his head over like he was actually trying to read the words on the page. Was it an act of habit or want for closeness? That was the question.

"What are you researching?" Grayson inquired.

Ryker broke from his fixation on the book in his hands to look up at Grayson with an unseeable smirk. "Business techniques."

Grayson laughed at the response shaking the couch as he fell against the back of it. It was contagious, within seconds Ryker found himself laughing alongside Grayson. He closed his book with a small slam and allowed himself to just laugh without a care of what he had been searching for before.

"You dick, you're distracting me!" Ryker hit his friend's arm with his hand. Grayson just continued to laugh, Ryker's annoyed words fueling the amusing aspect for the laughing. So in response Ryker just sighed, leaning forward to trade the book in his hands for the laptop that sat on the coffee table already running.

"Maybe you shouldn't let yourself get distracted so easily." Grayson responded. The overture of the movie begins to lightly play, interrupting the laughing fits and Ryker's growing irritation.

Ryker didn't satisfy Grayson by giving him a response letting his attention get taken by the program running already. A green bar moving across his screen but not filling it in. Large green words sat on the screen.

`Download 76%`

Ryker frowned, pushing the white with red cane from its spot on the table the computer was put down beside it. Legs pulled up to his chest Ryker pulled an in reach blanket close to him At least he had a little bit of time to watch a movie.

Chapter 6

"Hey, don't worry, it's pretty simple."

New hires weren't generally Ryker's issue, he wasn't the manager in charge of hiring them. By the time they got a position they were already assigned someone to shadow for the first few days. Of course this morning when one of his employees happened to be late and he found himself gravitating towards the panicking kid. They were so new they didn't even know how to clock in, their head jerking side to side in hopes to find someone else checking in somewhere. It made Ryker sad seeing everyone else just watch this kid and do nothing to help him. He looked close to tears and they just stood there.

Besides, helping was a distraction from the fact he wished to go home and check his computer for the hundredth time. He had downloaded everything, he just needed to go through it all. Nos was not the time to do that though, rent was still due at the end of the month so he had to get to his shifts properly. And in the end early shifts were the easiest to deal with.

"Just type in the number behind your name tag. It will be your number for pretty much anything so if you just memorize that everything will get pretty easy really quick."

Ryker stepped up, holding his name tag in view of the new kid so he could see the numbers that sat below the pin. The kid gave quick nods in response. With shaking hands the kid pulled off his name tag and slowly began typing the number on the back.

"Aww look at the newbie with our grumpy manager. I think we may actually get to see him smile next. Wouldn't we be so lucky?" Someone joked in the most mocking voice they could conjure without a laugh.

"You would be lucky to keep your job if you continue to talk."

Ryker didn't even have to turn around to know who stood there—probably leaning obnoxiously on the counter behind the front desk—watching him. Actually, Ryker would prefer the word stalking. He knew it wasn't the correct word for the situation but he could pretend— especially to make Marc mad.

"How did I end up with you working during my shift, Marc?" He couldn't just stand there forever though, so he might as well get over it and turn to face his employee who more than likely held a stupid grin on his face. Which Ryker was exactly right about when he saw Marc, face in his hands and elbows resting on the counter.

"Seriously, why are you here all the time?"

"Despite how badly I want to guess you are in love with me and you make the schedules which most of the time forces me to be here, we both know I'm just poor and work all the shifts I can." Marc stood up straight, walking to meet with Ryker when he emerged from the host booth. He elbowed Ryker. "Besides, we know about you and that roommate of yours."

"So you know that Grayson isn't dating because he just broke up with his boyfriend last month?" Ryker questioned. "And that I don't date people."

Marc held his hands up to the side, a physical sign of a surrender to the verbal attack, "Okay I didn't know about the first thing, but are you really telling me you never had a crush on him. You've known him for so long and never had feelings?"

Of course, people never understand our situation. Topics like this have changed so much over time. Almost forty years ago people like them were still fighting for their rights and worrying about them getting taken away now but things have mellowed out. People are more accepting, but there are still a lot who were not. You could never be too careful about what you say. People take any chance to make opinions out of nothing but a little bit of overheard conversation.

"Once we had been friends for a while, yes." Ryker answered truthfully. Maybe if he just gave someone the truth he would have one less person asking questions. Besides he has known for a while, maybe he could let one person outside of his apartment learn things about him. "But then it kind of went away, I moved on and I'm glad I did. Grayson is my brother and neither of us want anything to change that."

Marc let out a small *oh*.

"Uh, Mr. Griffin." Ryker welcomed the excuse to stop looking at Marc's sorry expression. Perhaps he would thank the new hire for calling him over later but for now he had to deal with the person who called for him. The person with partially closed eyes, eyebrows drawn together, as they seemed to be in thought.

"What's going on?"

"There is a lady on the phone, she requested to speak with you. She wouldn't give me a name, just that she wanted to talk to Ryker Griffin and only him. She wasn't dealing with any arguments about it either."

Ryker could hear the words he wanted to say. *She's terrifying.*

Ryker grumbled as he walked to the phone. Customer complaints were his least favorite things to deal with at all but he hated it more in the morning. Why did everyone think it was a good idea to wait until early the next morning to complain to whoever was there?

Who could be calling for me right now?

He picked up the phone left on the host booth. "Hello, this is Ryker Griffin."

"Mr. Griffin, so nice to hear from you after so many years."

A shiver went down the manager's spine hearing the chilling woman's voice on the other end of the phone. After she had stopped giving orientations a few years back, he never expected to hear her speak directly to him ever again.

They owned the business, but they also hired people to run it so they never had to do anything with it.

Why is she calling? What does she want?

It was never good when she called, especially if it was actually her and not her assistant.

"Good morning Mrs. Sallow." Ryker glanced at his employees who grouped together near the counter to listen. Even with a glare and a wave of a hand to leave, they stayed put. Ryker rolled his eyes. *Idiots.*

"How can I assist you today Mrs. Sallow?"

"My family is celebrating, we need a table tonight at exactly seven." Mrs. Sallow stated. Flipping through their reservation it was easy to see they would have to move some things around but they could make it work.

"Okay, may I ask how many guests will be with you?" Ryker drummed his fingers on the host booth.

"There will be six of us. We prefer the table to be set with three chairs on each side of the table. Somewhere private if you know what I mean." Mrs. Sallow answered.

There was a moment of silence while Ryker wrote in the restaurant's reservation book, putting down the small details that they wanted so whoever was working tonight wouldn't mess up. But when someone did speak it was Ryker who broke the silence. Instead it was broken with a click of a tongue and Mrs. Sallow's voice. "And we want you on the floor caring for us."

Ryker looked up, like there was a person standing there for him to speak to. "I'm sorry Mrs. Sallow but my shift end—"

"Pay yourself however much extra you want,

we want you. You understand how to care for us and we wouldn't take anyone else." Mrs. Sallow responded. "So, what's it going to cost us?"

~~

"The tables aren't aligned!"

A groan escaped Ryker who seemed as though he was running around like a chicken without a head trying to make everything run smoothly. From the lighting on the table, alignment of the table, and having all silverware and plates set up before the special guests even arrived. It needed to be perfect. *They* needed it to be flawless.

"Ryker, stop worrying so much. It's fine. You don't need to act like a mad man." Marc's shift was over, it had been over for almost two hours but when he was offered pay for overtime he stayed to help set everything up and give Sofi the rundown of the bar drinks already known that the Sallow family orders. Guess it was good that they tended to order the same things every single time.

"Seeing as it is not your job we are worrying about, maybe we should let me act like a mad man."

"You've been serving since you were fifteen and a manager since you were seventeen. Stop acting like this family is any different than any of the other times you have served people."

Marc was right, this shouldn't be that different, even if they were the Sallow family. During his first year of working here he must have served them specifically a dozen times. He was a teenager back then, he had a lot more experience now. Even if it wasn't exactly perfect everything would be fine.

"Speaking of the Sallow family," Marc gestured with his head to the front door. "Incoming."

Ryker turned to face the doors. They swung open, the bell above jingling through the strangely quiet restaurant, pairs walking in one after another. Mr. and Mrs. Sallow led the group forward and to the host booth, following behind them were their own children, lastly were a pair of people Ryker thought were familiar but couldn't place why. One was an older looking gentleman, the other was a woman whose eyes remained down on the ground, careful to not step on the feet in front of her. All of them were dressed up, the men in black suits and ties, the women were all in dresses with the two older ones wearing darker reds and the little Sallow girl wearing a soft pink with a big white bow and blue plastic glitter childrens heels.

I wish I saw the fight that went down to get to the agreement for her to wear those.

Ryker stood up straighter, wiping his hands against the nonexistent wrinkles in his dress shirt and pants. Taking in a deep breath the manager crossed through the dining area to the host booth.

A glare pointed towards him by one of the guests during the short walk it took for him to get to the host booth. He didn't respond with his own though, instead letting his eyes land on the hostess that was going to take them to a table.

"I can handle this one." Ryker spoke to the hostess who was fumbling with menus, not taking widened eyes off tonight's special guests. He smiled, lips pressed tightly together, and gathered 5 adult menus then a single childrens one—grabbing a few extra packs of crayons so all the colors they had would be present.

"We have your table set up in a more private area." Ryker led the group away from the booth. He fell into taught dialogue, explaining where they would be sitting even if they already knew. "There are no windows so you will have your requested privacy."

Ryker worked swiftly, placing the menus at the table the Sallows and their guest sat in whichever seats they decided to claim—Ryker even walked over to push in some of the chairs like he was taught. The two Sallow children and their mother sat on one side leaving Mr. Sallow and their guests on the other. This was for business talk, most likely putting the three with the most power together in a corner to discuss and putting those the most affected in the other corner like a child in time out.

"Can I start you off with something to drink?" Ryker asked. By this point almost all of the adults had already begun to sift through the menu. There was one person who did not but their gaze hadn't moved off Ryker pretty much the entire time.

"What do you have?" The older gentleman asked.

"Well.." Ryker glanced over the table, watching the head pointed his way snap to the girl coloring instead. With a polite smile Ryker listed off the types of drinks they served—alcoholic and not.

He just had to make it through this night without any issues but how was he supposed to do that with the pair of eyes trying to burn holes into the back of his head? Maybe he just had to figure out a way to get rid of the watchful eyes.

"Perhaps we should begin discussing this wedding."

The older gentleman spoke the moment Ryker had taken a step away from the table to put their drink order in. Ryker glanced back at the table, luckily for him the bar wasn't too far away from it which just made it so much easier for him to listen to them. In fact most of the diners in the restaurant went silent to stare at the Sallows when they arrived. Not a single one seemed able to draw their eyes off the famous family once they arrived.

"Yes, let's discuss it." Mrs. Sallow agreed. "We wish for Alexander and Selene's wedding to go perfectly. How can we make that happen?"

Oh, this is going to be fun.

The bell over the door jingled as it swung open. The manager's head snapped in that direction and instantly recognized the bright grin from ear to ear of the person who had entered the building. Dressed in their most casual pair of jeans and graphic shirt, followed in by someone in tan shorts and flowy pine green tank top.

"Grayson." Ryker mumbled.

Okay, this wasn't going to be fun anymore.

What is he doing here? I thought he was staying home. Ryker thought to himself.

He wasn't supposed to be here, but neither were the Sallows.

Ryker excused himself from the bar while Marc worked to prepare the numerous drinks that would definitely take a moment. He crossed through the restaurant and to the table one of their hostess was setting up Grayson Finch and a guest he had brought with him, it was some girl Ryker knew he should recognize but didn't.

After checking behind him to see if anyone was watching, Ryker pulled his phone from his apron pocket checking it for any warning texts or a notification already set because of a planned reservation that he should have known about and forgotten. But his phone displayed a sad lack of messages. The last notification he got being from his weather app.

Seriously, what was he doing here? Why now?

"Gray?" Ryker snapped his name, getting an instinctual head turn towards himself. "What are you doing here?"

"I'm just getting some food with a friend." Grayson responded, shrugging at the question with an obvious answer to it. "Is there something wrong with that? I thought you said it was okay for me to bring people at any time."

"Can we talk a little bit more privately?" Ryker questioned. Fingers tapped against uniform regulated pants with no pattern to it.

Grayson nodded, barely able to get up out of his seat before Ryker harshly took grasp of his arm and pulled him to the close hall. The only things back there were the break room, storage room, and electrical room. Next break wasn't for fifteen minutes so they should be alone for a little while. Luckily, this conversation shouldn't take long and even if it did employees couldn't go on break without manager permission and as the manager of the day they had to ask him. At least he was manager of the day until he went off shift then it switched over to his coworker Alice.

Grayson tilted his head, furrowing his eyebrows, looking at Ryker. "What's going on?"

The dull flickering lights of the hall and the minimal distinctions between everything probably made it even harder for Grayson to figure out what was going on. Based on the lighting he could sometimes make out outlines or shapes, but this was no good lighting. Ryker should have known that.

"The restaurant has pretty important people eating here right now and it is really nerve wracking for everyone I think." Ryker said.

He wished to be able to tell Grayson everything. Tell him about Alexander and everything he was doing, tell him about the secrets he knew of the Sallow family, the engagement he overheard, he just wanted to tell him about every detail of life. But he couldn't do that. There was so little he could tell him in the first place and he hated every second of it. But there were some things he could tell Grayson.

"It's the Sallows and for some reason they wanted me as their server. They care about nothing but me being the one to wait on them and serve them tonight."

"That's good, isn't it?" Grayson asked. "People don't request certain staff members for no reason. It means they like you!"

Ryker scoffed. "Or they are thinking about firing me. That's honestly more likely than anything else. They just needed to come up with an excuse to and if I do bad this will be it, I will be out. I can't lose my job. I need this job, we need me to keep this job."

Grayson rolled his eyes letting out a quiet *'dramatic'* before turning his attention completely back to Ryker's panicked state. The way he took rapid breathes, how his grasp on Grayson's arm seemed to tighten so his nails dug into his arm. Grayson attempted to pull away when he first felt it but stopped after his hand trailed up to find it was definitely Ryker's hand touching him.

"We won't have money or a way to pay rent. We can't keep asking your parents for money, I can't even pay them back as it is." Ryker continued to ramble. "What if they want you to go back to them? I don't have anywhere else to go! I can't be alone *again!*"

Grayson reached out right in front of him and got his hands to fall upon the sides of Ryker's face. Moving his thumb he felt the tears that were flowing down Ryker's cheeks. Ryker hated that he knew any of this. The secrets he tried to keep being found out.

"Hey, it's okay. They aren't going to fire you, my parents aren't going to try and force me to go home—even if they did, I'm an adult—and everything is going to be fine." Grayson spoke gently. He pressed his hands down harder, fingers curling slightly. "It's so fine that you are going to serve the crap out of that family, get your largest tip ever—maybe even a promotion—then you are going to come home and beat me at every game we own while we watch fantastic cooking shows."

Ryker chuckled. "You and I both know your cooking shows are crap."

A gasp escaped from Grayson, a laugh escaping through ruining its dramatics. He wiped away a line of tears from his friend's face. "We both know you love those shows. Now come on, you need to go back to your table. Show them what you can do!"

"I hate you." Ryker mumbled.

"Love you too." Grayson slid his hands down to grab Ryker's arm, pulling him out of their hidden corner of the restaurant. Once out in the open Grayson lightly shoved him forward, not having a good idea how far the nearest table was. "Now go on. Your fancy guests are waiting!"

~~

Ryker did everything he was trained to do. Falling back into the basic steps of serving and relying on old information about the Sallow family to assist him. With everything in an established flow it all fell into place for a smooth evening. The only issue appeared when the youngest Sallow child knocked over a drink. A simple fix with a new drink and a new menu to color. Everyone was happy again without any sign of not being happy in the first place.

Not only were they happy, he was too. The panic was gone and replaced with excitement over the information he had received. An engagement was in place between the Sallows and the daughter of a famous director. Entertainment, a field in which the Sallows barely had their claws dug into. It was all making sense, they wanted their son to marry the actress daughter of a well liked director to give themselves another hand up on the situation. They were always one step ahead weren't they?

So ahead that they only ended their own meal almost exactly five minutes after Ryker's roommate had left the restaurant. Ryker knew that, he had stared at his watch until he was called over by the Sallows so they could leave. Coincidence, right? It had to be.

Ryker was doing a last minute look through of the reservations for the night, having left the Sallows to finish their conversations and collect their things. No one else was up there so his full attention laid on the booth, meaning he saw when a page of color was slid up onto the counter.

He turned his head to the short young girl who stood there having just put her paper into his view. Picking it up in his hands he turned and knelt down in front of her.

"It's beautiful." Ryker spoke. His fingers traced over the random line of orange that went across the page that he didn't understand. Just because he did not understand that did not mean it wasn't important. In the end though, he would describe it as beautiful.

"I mades it. For you." She rocked on to her tip toes then back on to the heels of her feet, arms bent and fists placed on her sides with a large grin on her face.

"Olivia!" The girl turned back to be greeted by the disapproving look of her father.

Did she run off just to give this to me?

Ryker didn't get much time to think about it before the girl ran out of the building with her father leaving Ryker with the approaching Mrs. Sallow and her son.

"Thank you, you were great like always." Mrs.

Sallow said on their way out. She nudged her son with her elbow, a slight snap coming with her next words. "Give him his tip Alex."

Alexander Sallow straightened up, turning to face Ryker before he held a small wad of cash towards the manager. His eyes never moved to look at him but instead stayed in his family's general direction. "Thank you for your service, Mr. Griffin."

Ryker took the cash from his hand. "You're welcome, *Alex*."

He spotted the other hand which seemed to form a tight fist around the extra cloth of his pants leg which he balled up. A singular spot that faced away from everyone.

"It was a pleasure to serve you all." Ryker stated. *And it will be a pleasure to take you all down. To save the country. To save everyone.*

Chapter 7

After the stolen thumb drive data had taken forever to download onto Ryker's computer and that shift serving the Sallows he knew what he found hidden upon the drive was well worth the wait. The information on it he wasn't supposed to hold yet he did so carelessly and left it on his personal computer. Not that it truly mattered though as he wanted it for one reason and once he got it his presence in the apartment vanished.

Several days passed before he got anywhere with the information he had though. Ryker's days were full and his schedule hectic. Days taken over by work at the restaurant—it was strangely busier than usual since the Sallows last visit. And his nights were sleepless while he camped out at an abandoned movie set. The best part of the tiring day—the part he looked forward to the most—was the bored phone calls from Grayson.

"You're working another late night. Really?" Grayson complained over the phone. Ryker could hear multiple voices, they weren't so loud that he couldn't hear Grayson but he did hear them. Where was Grayson even at?

Well he looked forward to the phone calls until Grayson questioned his whereabouts with his own loneliness. In Rykers opinion it was probably the saddest part of the job he had chosen. Having to hide his life from the person he wanted to tell about it the most was hard. He thought about telling him multiple times but in the end the risks outweighed the reward.

"Yeah, I'm sorry but you know how this works." Ryker started his lie with an attempt of sadness lacing his voice. It was always harder to lie to Grayson than anyone else. "My coworker who was supposed to take my shift called out and the restaurant needs a manager so I have to close. I probably won't be home until eleven or twelve."

Grayson let out a very obvious whine over the phone, unpleased with the information he had just been given by his best friend. The whining told Ryker that Grayson had planned something which involved him.

"What did you need from me?" Ryker asked. Calloused fingers ran through his hair, elbow propped against the window.

He glanced over to his personless passenger seat which was being taken up by a picture he had lacked the ability to either leave at work without care or bring it inside of the apartment. Should he really care that much about a picture of mostly just colors?

"There was this stand up show I wanted to go see

but it's too far of a walking distance." Grayson said. His voice dropped down to a whisper. "And I have two tickets."

Ryker looked back up and out of the window. "I'm sure one of your multitude of other friends would love to go with you and drive. You were saying that you missed them since you all had to get new jobs. There is your excuse to see one of them again."

Grayson had started to talk again but Ryker didn't process any of his words as a figure moved towards the building on a hill he had been watching. He unbuckled his seat belt and climbed out of the car quickly.

"Hey, I've got to go. I'll call you later."

Ryker hung up the phone, slamming his car door closed before he started a quick walk towards the building. His recently thrifted black cargo pants and bomber jacket hid him in the darkness as he got near what should have been an abandoned building. In fact, it had been under construction for the past year. So why was someone here of all places?

The entrance to the building had been completely taken apart, drywall pulled off leaving foundation and insulation in the cold and breezy—and dark—room. The hall leaving the room was more put together starting with the walls fully being put together, it was still dark though. Flooring tiles were already put in but were also already dirtied with large boot prints. No doors were in their places yet but the prints never seemed to venture down those halls. He wanted to investigate them anyways but he had things he needed to do, so Ryker continued forward on the well traveled path. Someone had been coming in and out of here for a while, but what were they doing here?

Ryker continued his journey down the hall until a light began to glow in the distance, it flourished in the hall. His eyes began to burn but Ryker continued until he was entering a large, far from empty, room ducking around a running spout of water to get in. The door sat open, scratches laid against the frame where the lock would have been.

"What?" Ryker mumbled.

He crossed through the open space, spinning slowly as he surveyed everything in sight.

The room was large and filled with a variety of items including bookshelves that lined the far wall, a messy table in the middle under a long light with a crowbar leaning against it, and a covered whiteboard like shape in a corner. Not a single area seemed to have an item in place, not even the bookshelf seemed organized as Ryker got close by.

Ryker decided to go to the table first. He picked up a file that sat among the top of many stacks that had been placed. Flipping open the file he revealed the dark bolded title on the top of the paper.

`Myst Falls Staff`

"What the hell?" Ryker mumbled to himself. He flipped through a multitude of pages that had sat there stapled together. Different Myst Falls in different locations were all listed here with their staff members and positions. Full names, addresses to send their paycheck, emergency contacts, phone numbers, emails. It was all here.

Finally Ryker reached their own location.

Starting right under the title was a list of names.

```
Sofi Cruz        Waiter/Bartender
Marc Reed        Host/Bartender
Brooke Howell    Waiter
```

He slid his fingers slowly along the list reading over the names of all of his workers in almost no particular order with the jobs on the other end of the page, all until he found a name that had been highlighted near the bottom.

```
Ryker Griffin            Manager
```

That wasn't even the worse part, the part that scared him the most. The worst part was the sticky note next to his name labeled 'Non employees'

```
Grayson Finch            Roommate
```

"No."

This wasn't something that Ryker could leave here in the hands of that arsonist and killer. Not his own name, not his workers, not anyone who could have been in danger. None of this could be left behind.

Ryker quickly examined the room until he spotted a small gleaming light from an object further on to the table. He scooped it up, letting his thumb slide against the back gear and the lighter in hand made its faint click sound. A miniature fire formed from the top.

Ryker looked up into the open sky. "Sorry universe, but it has to be done."

And with an apology said Ryker held the paper into the fire watching it catch alight and the flame begin to rise. He wasn't going to let any of those other people get involved or hurt because of him—not now, and not ever.

"What are you doing?" Someone snapped.

Ryker twisted around his gaze, falling on a figure that stood in the doorway. A grin formed on his face before he spoke, "Alexander Sallow, nice to see you again."

Ryker threw the items in his hands into a trashcan next to the table without thinking twice, taking a few large steps forward and towards the man. Had he been in there the whole time?

"How do you know my name?" Alexander asked.

Ryker barely bit the tip of his tongue as he continued to smile at the man. His hand crept towards his back pocket, "You're kind of famous, all you stuck up Sallows are. Can't believe you don't even know that. Anyone in your position would recognize that."

"You never answered my first question."

A hum escaped Ryker. "Maybe the question should be what are you doing here?"

Heat rose from behind Ryker, his back warming up uncomfortably quickly.

"Once again you are on the wrong side. I'm not the bad guy here."

"You're a murderer."

"Am I? How are you any different than me?"

The heat became a painful burning. Ryker spun around to see a fire that had engulfed the table of papers. He jumped back, slapping the back of his burning clothes to try and end the flames and his own pain. A click seemed to echo over his panic and the crackling of the fire.

Ryker turned back towards Alexander who held a small burning match in his hand looking at Ryker with a frown.

"Sorry but I did what I had to." Alexander dropped the match to half a ring of liquid on the ground. It looked like water but with just a single moment of contact the ring erupted into flames. That definitely wasn't water.

Sirens blared through the unfinished building growing closer and closer. Ryker's head snapped around as he looked for an exit out of the place he was trapped inside. Fire blocked the only exit that Ryker knew and the way this situation looked was not good on him at all. All that was left were boarded up doors and the few holes in the ceiling above.

Alexander watched for a moment before turning to exit down the long hallway. "Hey, this way!"

"Crap!" Ryker exclaimed, he was trapped. Eyes darting around for any signs of hope. His eyes finally landed on a door across the room, it was boarded up with long pieces of wood. That was going to be his only chance out of here right now, he had to try to get out of here.

Ryker grabbed on to the cold crowbar that was laying against the table, running from his spot and towards the boarded up door. Reaching it within seconds he fell to his knees on the stone laid beneath him. Sliding one end under the tightly nailed in wood was hard to do in such little time. Prying and pushing it in there, pulling the skin of his palms against the rough metal just to get it in. But once he put all his weight on the tool and began removing it—silently begging to whatever was out there to help him—he heard cracking.

He stumbled back as half the wood split apart. "Yes!"

He got to work on getting the other boards off as rapidly as he could until the door was finally uncovered. Before going through the door he glanced back just in time for armed police to make their way down the hall and into the room.

"Police! Freeze!"

And he did the exact opposite of that.

Ryker threw the door open and sprinted from where he stood in search of any exit possible. There weren't many options and Ryker should know that, he had gotten ahold of the old blueprints of the building and the closest 'exit' wasn't the most preferred way. It may be the only way.

"Damn it." Ryker took the only turn he knew he needed. A large window came into his view. Oh Grayson was so going to kill him for this one.

Ryker ran straight to the window twisting to his side as he jumped, his body colliding with the glass and a loud shattering echoing in his ears. He fell onto the cold hard grass, rolling down and away from the building he had been previously trapped in. A gasp escaped him as heat and pain flooded his right side, blood dripped on to that small insignificant spot in the field.

A single click and Ryker was rolling on to his back to look at the person who stood above him, the barrel of a black gun pointed right at his face. His body hurt, especially his arm which burned from taking most of the pain and force in the collision. A warm liquid had started to soak through his clothes in spots, blood dripping down his arm and side.

"Made it past the police. Seems you are smarter

than you make yourself look." Alexander Sallow's words rang in Ryker's head.

"And it looks like you are just about as smart as you look." Ryker swung his legs, hitting into Alexander's hard. His legs ached with the feeling of the hit but with it Alexander went stumbling back giving Ryker enough time to jump to his feet. He reached for his weapon but did not find it anywhere. Had he dropped it somewhere? Where could it be?

One of his few rules, always have a weapon. Now he was breaking it himself.

"Not smart at all." Ryker continued.

His dominant arm still burned in pain so he stuck to swinging his leg towards the unready Alexander who's back had been turned. The surprise hit seemed to be what had done him in as he fell to the ground, the gun falling from his hand mere inches away.

Alexander reached for his weapon but Ryker was already there, placing his booted foot onto Alexander's outstretched wrist. Using his other foot, not bothering with caring for the weight on the other's joint, he kicked away the gun.

"Finally caught you, guess that means I'm bringing another person like you down. Just have to wait for the police now," Ryker said.

Ryker watched Alexander's fingers wiggle, hand trying to outstretch to the gun with futile attempts to get it still but with one arm pinned he had to pick what he risked more, the arrest or the harming of himself to just maybe escape.

"Now what?" Ryker asked.

An answer didn't come from Alexander but a ringing did come through in the otherwise silent area. Ryker felt the vibration in his pocket from his phone, he pulled the phone from his pocket and pressed the simple answer and speaker buttons but didn't take his eyes off of Alexander.

"Hello?"

"Is this Ryker Griffin?"

Ryker let out a small growl at the sound of his name being said out loud in front of Alexander. "Yes, this is he. Who are you? What do you want?"

"I'm calling from Horizon General Hospital with a patient here, Grayson Finch…"

Chapter 8

December 16, 2061

Ryker could never remember being in a hospital before in his life. He had never broken a bone, never needed a surgery, and he could only ever remember getting his vaccines and shots from random Minute Clinics right inside of random Targets within distance of whatever activity his busy mother had to complete that day. Those clinics never counted and even if they did those trips were fun—getting dropped off at Target to do whatever he wanted while his mom worked only to be picked up a few hours later on her break to get brought home.

December 16th was not a fun trip.

December 16th was supposed to be the first major high school holiday party Ryker had ever gotten to attend, and his best friend Grayson Finch was supposed to be joining him. They had been excited for weeks, being some of the few juniors to get invited, but it didn't go how they planned at all.

"Shouldn't something have been said by now?" Ryker paced in front of the uncomfortable white and gray-blue chairs that lined one of the bland walls of a hospital. The room smelt like disinfectant, he hated that smell, no place should smell so strongly like this.

"Honey, sit down, I'm sure you'll learn something about your friend soon." His mom said softly. She put on that dumb voice Ryker recognized as her sick or hurt child nurse voice. She was trying to be comforting but she wasn't being that at all.

"But should it be taking this long?" Ryker asked. "It wasn't that bad right? I.. I saw it. The car crash, I saw it. It couldn't have been that bad. Right?"

A wail echoed down a hallway, Ryker's head snapped in that direction in an instant, he knew who had just gone down that hall after arriving mere minutes ago. It seemed like something that came from the movies—the cry of someone's death. Tears settled in his eyes, holding his breath he listened to the cries until a woman and a man emerged from the hall.

Ryker looked back at his mother for a moment before turning his head back to see the man walking towards him as the woman walked towards the door in sobs. Ryker ran forward to close the distance between himself and the man.

"Is Grayson—"

"Room 219." The man said. Ryker looked back

at his mom—who nodded at him—one last time before walking towards the hall.

The first time Ryker could remember being in the hospital it wasn't even for himself. The first time he was in the hospital he was running to a room, throwing the door open without care until his eyes landed on the person who laid in the bed. An obnoxious patterned beep kept going as he entered, and his hatred for it grew.

"Alix?"

"Hey Gray." Ryker walked into the room.

"My sister, Circe, where is she?" Grayson asked.

Ryker froze in the middle of the room. He had met Circe on a few occasions, she was just a Freshman this year and had been so excited for the holidays with her friends. But she had been in the car? Why was she in the car?

Grayson turned his head towards Ryker's direction, opening his eyes to look at his best friend. "Ryker?! Where are you? I can't see you! Why can't I see you?!"

December 21, 2061

The first actual vacation Ryker was supposed to have since he was 10 years old—a trip to New York—was canceled at his own request. Instead he stayed at home mostly living inside one of those horrible hospital rooms with his best friend. He sat there holding Grayson's hand as long as he needed, through tests and diagnosis, all until this day.

"Your mom wants to know who you want to go with, her or your dad?" Ryker said, reading a message from

Grayson's phone which had been within Ryker's possession for the past five days.

Ryker stepped out of the hospital bathroom in his best suit which his mom happened to buy from the closet thrift store a few days prior. His eyes landed on Grayson dressed in a white suit standing in front of a mirror in the room. His hand was outstretched to feel the material where it sat.

"Gray?"

"It hurts." Grayson spoke up.

"What hurts?" Ryker asked. Any care of his about the question he was supposed to be getting answered was gone as he moved towards his friend. "Do I need to call a doctor? Do you need to si—"

"She's dead, like really dead." Grayson turned his head towards where he assumed his best friend stood based on his voice. Tears rolling down his cheeks, a fountain unable to be stopped. Ryker didn't try to correct the few inches off. "Ryker, my sister is dead and it's all my fault."

~~

In the end Grayson decided to ride in his fathers car with the other males in the family due to some sort of family tradition. Ryker rode with his mother to the burial but he didn't walk with her to the site and instead waited until a row of black cars arrived and a few people dressed in white got out of the vehicles. Only a select couple of those people moved towards the hearse that had been in the front. But Ryker only looked at one person.

"Ryker maybe it's best if you go ahe—"

Ryker ignored whoever tried to talk to him, he strode towards someone who was working on taking slow and cautious steps away from the recently parked car trying to slide their feet against the ground as a guide. The other riders had long got out and moved away to speak with the family leaving the final rider all alone.

"Grayson." Ryker called out. Grayson's head snapped his general direction.

"Alix." Ryker closed the space between them as quickly as he could, grabbing one of Grayson's hands to inform him that he was there. They were both right there together. "Alix, I can't do this. My dad and his dad are waiting. I'm supposed to carr- It's tradition but I can't do this."

Ryker frowned. "Hey, it's okay. She would want you more than anyone else, we both know that. You weren't the one to hit someone else, okay? Remember that."

"But I brought her, I just got my license and it was icy. If I didn't bring her—" Grayson choked back a sob, his head falling down and his body shook. "I can't even see the path. She's my sister and I can't even do this last thing for her. It's just us!"

Ryker placed his free hand on his friend's shoulder, giving it a small squeeze for him to look up once again. "If it's okay with your family, I'll help."

"What?" Grayson asked.

"Your family has always been like my family. I want to help, please, I'll help and lead you so you can bury your sister."

"Please."

Present Day

Ryker had been to the hospital more times then he cared to count now—not that he even tried to count every. But this time he couldn't help but only think about that very first time where he was forced to sit in the hospital waiting room since he arrived. He was given the basic information, as Grayson's emergency contact, when he arrived and for the first time he felt like he was that 16 year old boy standing in the waiting room anticipating that cry of death all over again.

There had been a car crash. The first car Ryker could think about Grayson getting in with someone other than himself or his family behind the wheel and Grayson's in the hospital again. All he had wanted to do was watch stand up. How was this fair? How was any of this fair?

Ryker looked up at the sky calling out to whatever might be listening in the universe today. *I'm the one going out and getting myself in danger constantly. So why him? What did he do to deserve this?*

The nurses at the desk said they would give him information whenever they could—at first they had believed he was the one who was going to be a patient with injuries he wasn't willing to explain—but around the half hour point he was done waiting. He couldn't just sit here as they talked so calmly with one another and the people that came in only to get sent to the waiting area as well. He wasn't going to just sit here any more.

Ryker got to his feet and started to stride towards the desk when a hand wrapped itself around his arm. He spun around on his heel instantly, the grip stung wasn't tight at all so it was simple to turn himself to face the person who stood there—Alexander Sallow.

"Sit back down, Ryker."

"What are you doing here, Sallow?" Ryker snapped. How dare he come here at this time? Ryker could have waited and let the police get him but instead he let him go and came to the hospital alone. He had been alone.

"Relax." Alexander released his grip on Ryker's arm, gesturing towards the chairs of the waiting room. "We are both just humans tonight."

Alexander gestured towards the chairs once again so finally Ryker walked over there to sit down, Alexander following and taking the seat next to him. Both looked forward at the surprisingly unbusy room. There were just a few people who sat across the room but they were busy with their phones and selves or their own nerves to notice what was going on around them.

"What do you want?" Ryker asked.

"To talk." Alexander answered with a hum following after. His eyes moved around the room, his head going with it. "After you let me go to come here I thought that was the least we could do."

Two people walked out of a side hallway and towards the desk blocking the nurses view of the waiting room for just a moment. Ryker slowly slid his hand along the jeans he had changed into in his car, a knife lived inside the pocket so if he could just—

A rough calloused hand slammed harshly on top of his own trapping his hand against his upper thigh. Ryker turned his head to look at Alexander who spoke. "Don't try it. There is no reason for anyone to get hurt right now."

"If that is true why are you here then?" Ryker asked.

"To give you an offer." Alexander looked over at Ryker with a frown. He was putting on an act. No one could hear them but they could definitely see them right now. A concerned friend with another concerned friend, that's what Alexander wanted to be seen as least. Good publicity for himself in the end. "A temporary truce. Take care of your friend for a little bit. Neither of us will make a move. Deal?"

"Why?" There were thousands of ways Ryker knew he could have responded but instead he stuck to the simple one. A singular word to mean almost everything he had wanted to say.

"Because like I said before, we are human. So I'm offering you two weeks. Get your friend settled back in and taken care of."

Ryker turned his head towards Alexander. "Are you even aware of what is going on with your own company or does this take up all your time? Your family isn't made of good people."

"Watch your mouth." Alexander responded. He released Ryker's hand, getting to his feet. Ryker jumped to his feet, his left hand creeping towards the knife he held. He doubted that Alexander would try anything. "Two weeks, yes or no."

Ryker bit down on his lip. "Fine, two weeks."

Alexander nodded. "Then I'm ending this for now. Enjoy it all while you can."

As Alexander began to walk away Ryker slipped his hands into his jean pockets, the fingers on his right hand tapped against a plastic object that sat inside. He looked down, pulling an item out into view.

"Alexander." Ryker called out. Alexander turned back just as Ryker threw the item in his hand towards him. It was caught easily by the other.

"What is this?" Alexander held up the item.

"You should know, it's your own flash drive." Ryker responded. He fell back into his seat. "I added some stuff on it, maybe you should take a look at it yourself. Perhaps you'll learn something new that you need to."

Alexander didn't respond to the comment, instead he just shoved the flash drive into the pockets of his dress pants. Running his hands over the slight wrinkles that formed from sitting down. He turned back to Ryker once again, stepping away and leaving Ryker to wait in his silence again.

~~

A couple minutes later—it felt like hours—a nurse came out and retrieved Ryker from the waiting room showing him down one of the halls he knew way too well in his life and to a room with a cracked open door. Ryker could hear the sound of a TV playing from inside, some obnoxious judgy voice as a man talked about someone's creation while it was still being made.

"Thank you." Ryker said to the nurse before he walked to the door and pushed it the rest of the way open to reveal the bland hospital room. "Gray?"

A head snapped in his direction, instantly a hug smile settled on Grayson's face. "Alix! You're here, finally."

"They wouldn't tell me anything until just a few minutes ago, give me some grace." Ryker earned a chuckle from Grayson. It was music to his ears just to listen to Grayson laugh right now. He always seemed to be able to laugh at the worst, yet best, times. It just made his heart ache to hear it right now. "Tell me what happened."

"The nurse put on the TV, do you think she knows I can't actually see it?" Grayson didn't respond to what Ryker wished for him to.

Ryker crossed through the room and settled in a chair near the bed. "They have access to your medical records, of course they know. Besides you and I both know you enjoy listening to the shows so stop avoiding the topic. What happened?"

He needed Grayson to get to the point instead of tiptoeing around it like it didn't exist. Ryker needed to know who he needed to kill and if they were in this hospital for very easy access.

"But it's no fun watching the bad cooking shows if you can't see the things they make on the bad cooking shows."

Again, avoiding the topic.

"Gray." Ryker snapped.

Grayson went quiet for a moment, his head tilted down and his hands fidgeted with the blanket laying over his lap. Fingers running over the edges of the blanket, eyes not able to make a connection with another. "I heard it was a drunk driver. They were leaving the bar nearby and didn't see Kaley and me. Guess luckily for us they hit the back more than us."

"Driver survive?" Ryker asked.

"Yeah, apparently he walked off the scene unhurt." Grayson said. "Police found him a block away."

"I'm going to kill them." Ryker snapped. Hands curled into fists, knuckles turning white.

That got Grayson turning his head with eyes narrowed into a glare. "No you aren't. I'm fine, Kaley is fine, you are definitely fine. No one is being killed."

"I could kill him." Ryker mumbled, crossing his arms and sinking down in his chair. Grayson scoffed at his friend's empty threat, or believed to be an empty threat.

Grayson scooted over on his bed not caring about hospital rules too much as he patted the now unoccupied spot beside him. "Come watch this show with me, I need you to tell me how awful these cakes are."

Ryker sighed but walked to the bed to climb in next to his best friend to start the game called 'Describe that cake.' Even as Grayson laughed and mocked him for his bad impressions of the judges, Ryker somehow never won.

December 17, 2061

Ryker slept on the gray couch in the hospital room.

His parents had allowed it, telling the nurses and doctors he was family, allowing him to stay and not be forced to go home and wait for his mom to be able to drop him off. He didn't have his own car, he and his mom couldn't afford it, but if he did this would still have been the situation. Maybe he could trade his vacation money for a car.

Nevertheless, Ryker woke up before Grayson did, but in all fairness he was no doubtably high on painkillers. But he shouldn't have to be on painkillers in the first place. He shouldn't have to cry himself to sleep about his sister, or worry about not being able to ever see again. None of this should be happening. If only the city was safe.

Ryker looked across the room at his best friend.

He'll make it safe, even if it's the last thing he does.

Chapter 9

"I don't need a babysitter, Alix."

Ryker and Grayson entered their joint apartment with one another, Ryker slammed the door closed behind them as Grayson began to cross the apartment and away from his best friend. Ryker ventured into the kitchen instead of following after, but still had an almost perfect view of the living room where Grayson walked.

"Tell me that when you don't smell like a hospital." Ryker responded. "You were in a car accident, I have the right to worry."

Grayson let out a scoff, falling on to the couch he had walked too with a bounce. "I had minor injuries, they only made me go because I blacked out a little bit and they were concerned."

"Ah yeah, *concerned* is the key word there." Ryker pulled two bowls from the upper cabinets and placed them on to their counter. A groan escaped him from his sore arms, he had expected them to burn or hurt more but weirdly it didn't make him feel that much different then how he had been feeling recently. He then began his search in their cupboard for chips, they had to have some.

Ryker took a moment to peek into the living room, it was just in time to see a gingerly folded blanket get pulled off of the back of the couch where it had previously laid. Ryker chuckled, Grayson hadn't even lifted his head up to try and put himself in an easy position for laying the blanket over himself. That just happened to provide Ryker the entertainment of seeing Grayson's slightly flailing limbs to finish his poorly planned wants.

"You were in the hospital Grayson." Ryker went back to his chip gathering before he went to pour them into the horrible green colored bowls they owned. Mixing the spicy, as well as the more sour chips, into one bowl and then just filling the second one with the remains of the spicy bag.

"And they still worried less than you." Grayson yelled.

Ryker scoffed. "Yeah okay, guess I won't get you chips then if I should worry about you less."

Grayson's head finally made its appearance over the back of the couch, his head turned towards where the kitchen and by default where Ryker was standing. He frowned, Ryker could assume it was in hopes that he would see it and pity him enough to not sacrifice the chips.

"You know, you're a whiny person when you want something." Ryker commented.

"Would you give me things if I wasn't?"

"No." Ryker answered. *Yes.*

He scooped the bowls off the counter and walked into the living room with his offering for his roommate. Grayson's frown was replaced with a large grin when the bowl got shoved into his hands. He fell back down to laying on the couch with his trophy of a chip monstrosity in his hands.

Grayson continued smiling, it felt like a silent movie playing that Ryker didn't want to look away from. Despite everything he seemed genuinely happy, and that is how Ryker wanted him to be for a while.

"Gray, if we could do anything within the next two weeks what would you want to do?"

"What do you mean?" Grayson grabbed the two different types of chips he had and bit into them. Ryker turned his head away, his nose scrunching with disgust at his best friend's decision. He could get behind many things Grayson did but not mixing sour and spicy chips. It was horrendous.

Ryker sighed, placing his bowl of chips on to the table next to a folded up cane and a picture sitting on top of a bought frame that he gave up trying to open earlier. "I'm taking a break from work for a little bit. I've been working too much and there is this thing in two weeks that I know is going to take up a lot of time."

"Are we talking about work or something else, Alix?" Grayson questioned.

"There is nothing else I would be talking about." Ryker sat down in the armchair in their living room. "I've noticed how much I've been working and how little I've been hanging out with you, okay? So just tell me what you want to do."

Grayson frowned but looked away almost like he was pondering the idea of what he might want to do. "What is the limit for this?"

Ryker shrugged. "Whatever you want. I'll wait for you to come tell me what it is. I'll be in my room."

Grayson gave a small nod letting Ryker take his lone bowl of chips out of the room and towards his bedroom for a little bit of quiet time.

~~

Ryker had fallen onto his bed, head buried in a book series he had never quite gotten the chance to read before, when Grayson popped his head in and spoke. "I think I know where I want to go."

"Oh really?" Ryker asked. He put his book down on the bed next to the hideous green bowl that was on his bed, giving his complete attention to his best friend who hopped their way into the doorway. "Where?"

"Do you remember that trip we took in Miss. Anaya's class?" Grayson question. He reached out and poked a bobble head that had randomly made its home on Ryker's desk before crossing his arms. He leaned against the wooden frame of the door, kicking one of his feet out going forward and back on the carpet in the room.

Grayson continued. "That one in the 6th grade?"

"Yeah to the aquarium. You were so scared of

the sharks that you refused to even walk down the hall
they were in until my group came and I held your hand
the whole way down it." Ryker responded. Red quickly
emerged taking over Grayson's face—dominating his
cheeks and tips of his ears the most.

"I only held your hand because it meant I could
look at the ground and you would guide me." Grayson
crossed his arms and frowned as he looked towards his
friend. "Besides, you didn't have to bring it up."

Ryker chuckled. Swinging his legs off his bed he
stood up and began the small journey across the room to
where Grayson now leaned in the doorway. "Why do you
bring up the trip?"

"That's where I want to go, the aquarium."

"Deciding to face your fear of sharks today?" Ryker
teased.

"It's completely rational! Plus I was a kid, I'm not
afraid of them anymore." Grayson yelled, stomping his
foot. Ryker laughed at the childish act of his friend. "So can
we go or not?"

"Yeah sure, I'll buy us some tickets and we can
go tomorrow." He wondered what could have brought the
sudden idea to Grayson's mind to go there of all places.
After a car accident Ryker expected the last place he would
want to go is a place with something he feared.

Was fear why?

Grayson threw his hands up into the air with his
victory over his best friend. A smile made its way onto
his face screaming his enjoyment and pleasure that was
probably going through his mind. He bounced where he

stood. "And you can see the fish and everything around."

Ryker frowned. "Gray this is supposed to be something you want to do, it's not for me."

"I know that, just make sure we can go see the dolphin show and I promise I'll be happy. I love sitting in the splash zones for those things." Grayson tried to reassure him. His hands on his hips, standing up on the tips of his toes when he spoke.

Grayson turned and walked out of the room leaving Ryker not being able to say another word, or at least he didn't try to say another word to him. Instead a loud sigh just escaped from Ryker before he walked to his desk to try and get the tickets for the aquarium. If this is what Grayson wanted then that's what he was going to get.

"Why can't you be easy Gray?" Ryker mumbled to himself. He pulled up the site for the aquarium and began to scroll. "You are supposed to be making yourself happy, not me."

Ryker stopped scrolling as he reached an activity linked on to the site.

Perfect.

~~

Ryker couldn't get online tickets for the next day but Ryker did get some for a few days later into the week. Grayson was happy to wait, being content with days filled with listening to new songs, going shopping, and anything else Ryker could think of them doing for the next two weeks. All of it just built up to the day and the event

Grayson had begged for.

"Alix, they said they were about to feed the sharks. Shouldn't we go? It could be fun." Grayson pulled at his friend's hand to try and stop him from bringing them in the opposite direction then they had been directed. His voice had shook as he spoke about a certain type of sea animal, one he definitely wasn't excited to see.

"Be patient. I have a surprise for you." Ryker said. He pulled against his best friend's tugging and brought them towards a different hallway. Arching over them were glass walls revealing the tanks full of water and sea life. Blue lights shone through the water reflecting the gentle ripples on to what would have been the otherwise dark floor

"Alix, it's dark."

Ryker didn't register the lack of interlacing with his hand until Grayson spoke up. A curse escaped from him as he stepped towards Grayson who had frozen at the halls entrance. "Sorry."

Ryker took cautious care in the taking of Grayson's hands in his own, leading him deeper down the hall until stopping them in the middle of their path to their planned destination. He looked up into the water.

"Hey Gray, look up."

He watched the water above as fish swam by before a shadow loomed over them blocking out some of the light with its large gray body. Grayson let out a soft 'woah' as he stared up into the water. His eyes had widened with the giant smile that had landed on his face.

Ryker squeezed Grayson's hands for his attention. "Congratulations, you've officially stood under a shark."

"What?!" Grayson yelled.

"Yeah, that was a shark." Ryker said.

Grayson let out a laugh. "I just stood under a shark. A fucking shark!"

Ryker laughed with his friend as he continued to pull him down the hallway and through another doorway. The light brightened in the room that wasn't completely empty but it wasn't too crowded. Ryker glanced around the room until his eyes landed on a glass tank with no sort of lid on the top.

"Come on." Ryker tugged Grayson towards the tank, letting go of one of his hands to place it on the edge of the tank as a new support. He glanced down into the tank of water and more importantly at the animals that swam through the water below them.

"What's going on?" Grayson asked. Water lapped against the side of the tank hitting against Grayson's finger tips.

"Just trust me for once." Ryker responded. He let go of Grayson's hand and instead let his own wrap around Grayson's wrist to direct him. Together they lowered their hands into cold water together, Grayson putting his trust in Ryker completely.

"Just hold your hand there for a second, Gray."

Ryker watched as a creature in the water moved towards Grayson's hand, beginning to glide under it. Once its head got out of the way Ryker lowered Grayon's hand deeper into the water letting his fingertips brush delicately against the grayish figure below.

Grayson tried to hold back a laugh but it just

escaped him as he pulled his hand abruptly away from the creature that had been there.

"Was that a stingray?" Grayson asked.

"It's a touch pool." Ryker didn't exactly answer the question. "I thought with the way the lights are you would be able to make out where things were and even then you at least got a chance to touch them."

"You know, sometimes I love you."

Ryker rolled his eyes. "I'm well aware. Now come on, let's go touch some animals."

Grayson clapped his wet hands together as he and Ryker began their adventure to touch the creatures of the touch pool before their planned visit to one of the few dolphin shows that day.

~~

"I can't believe I actually got to touch a shark." Grayson spoke. He laid on the grass of a hill uncaring about the wet and coldness beneath him as he laid there with his best friend. Their hands sat between them and smiles laid on their faces as they looked up at the cloud gliding through the air above them.

Neither Ryker nor Grayson really cared about going to the other things—with the exception of the dolphin show. Grayson had been captivated by the touch pool and the glass hall he had named "The Shark Hall". He almost missed the dolphin show, if Ryker had not pulled him from his entertainment he would have missed it and sitting in the splash zone.

And while Grayson had been focused on every animal around him Ryker found himself staring right at his friend. The way his smile seemed to light up the whole room. Even when the dolphin show had to be pushed back to give the dolphins a longer break he just was so happy. Could he ever not be?

So worth it.

"We did this in 6th grade too. Laying on this very hill exactly like this." Ryker spoke up through Grayson's excitement. He reached out and grabbed his friend just to know Grayson was actually there and even potentially listening.

"Do you remember that?" Ryker asked.

"Wait really?" Grayson turned his head towards his best friend.

"Yeah, it was actually three of us." Ryker responded. "You were so afraid Miss. Anaya would suspend us that you almost went back and turned us in. But she didn't even know we were gone."

Grayson laughed. "How did you convince me not to tell?"

"I didn't. We have another friend, they convinced you." Ryker responded. "Honestly I was pretty sure you had a crush on them and that's the only reason that you stayed with us."

Grayson sat up quickly with news he hadn't expected to hear that day. He remembered that day and the person who had been with them. How did he not think of this earlier? "Oh my god, I remember her—"

"Him." Ryker corrected. "He goes by he and him

now."

"Oh okay." Grayson nodded, he did frown slightly but Ryker expected it was because he felt bad rather than anything else. "Do you know what he goes by now?"

Ryker watched as a cloud shaped like a distorted heart began to move across his field of vision. "Alexander Sallow."

Chapter 10

The sun rose, colors speckled through the room shooting out from the orange and pink jellyfish suncatcher hanging from the window. Stuffed animals had fallen to the ground last night and had yet to be picked up and thrown back onto the bed.

"Ryker, you're going to make your friends late!"

"I'm coming!"

A young boy pulled a hat over his hair which was fluffed from trying to dry it after an early morning shower. With a last second glance in the mirror he approved of his red and black flannel, and his blue jeans. He snatched his bag from the ground, running out of his room and towards the front door that his mom waited with, one of his classmates—a girl from his class.

"Yeah Ryker, you're going to make us late." She teased. Her hair had recently been cut and when Ryker looked at her all he could think was at least he didn't have to watch her take children's scissors to her hair this time. "Come on Ryke!"

A hand was held out for him to take, a friendly smile waiting for him. He took the hand with a firm grip. His friend tugged him from the doorway and out of the house. Ryker got a quick goodbye out to his laughing mom before the two broke off into a run heading straight to their bus stop.

"Guys hurry up! We are going to be late!"

"Calm down Gray, it's right there!" Ryker gestured wildly at the bus as they just barely made it before the

bus doors opened up. How long had it been sitting there waiting? Couldn't be long if Grayson was so worried about being late. But Grayson tended to get worried a lot about such little things like this.

The bus driver had her normal bright smile on as she looked at them. "Oh look at my favorite best friend trio. Just barely on time, Mr. Griffin and Ms. Sallow."

~~

"Did you enjoy the aquarium, Gray?"

The click of his turn signal resonated through the car as they were forced to sit at one of the most obnoxious red lights in the city—one that they had just barely missed making it through. It didn't mean anything other than they were just stuck sitting in wet clothes a little bit longer than they wanted with no idea when the universe—the traffic lights—would let them go.

"Gray?"

Grayson sat—tilted away from Ryker—in the passenger seat, silent until this point with only music to fill the awkward silence. He had slipped on his normal bright red sunglasses—to keep his eyes from hurting even more than they were with the sun against them—making it hard to see what he was focusing on but Ryker knew his attention was stuck on what sat outside of the window as they drove. Or at least that was what he believed.

"Why do you keep lying to me?" Grayson asked. "I know you've been lying about going to the restaurant. I went there during one of your *shifts* and no one had seen you all day. What have you been lying to me about?"

"What?" Ryker glanced over at his best friend after the *suddenness* of his question and accusations but the light flashed to green so he couldn't look that way for too long. "What are you talking about?"

A car behind him honked, forcing his foot down on to the gas before he made too many city drivers mad.

"I've always been at the restaurant when I told you I would be there." Ryker continued.

His hands turned to pale on the steering wheel as he gripped it. For once he was happy Grayson wouldn't be able to see something he was doing—the simple tell to signify his anger. An aggressive action against the inanimate object that it was. An aggressive action he found happening more often than intended but it was one of the only things he knew he didn't have to hide.

"You've always been good at lying to me Ryker, and I hate it." Grayson shifted in his seat, spinning himself around to face Ryker who couldn't look at him. "I've never been sure about any of my thoughts before this moment but this time I am. You sneak out all night, come home hurt, and act like I am clueless when I'm not. I want the truth, what's going on? What are you not telling me?"

"Nothing."

"Liar!" Grayson exclaimed. He hit his hands against the center console, jumping with his movement before turning to slouch in his seat. His arms crossed over his chest until his sunglasses started to slide towards the tip of his nose and he had to push them back up.

"I hate you and all this crap you pull. I hate it,

Ryker!"

An invisible knife was taken and plunged into Ryker's heart as he heard the words that spilled from his friend's mouth. He knew why the harsh words were being said, the dishonesty Ryker had been letting pass without a second thought, but he still had a right to hate it. A right to keep Grayson out of harm's way without feeling guilty about it. It was all to keep Grayson safe after all.

"I'm sorry Gray."

"Why can't you just tell me?" Grayson asked. "I'm your best friend. I'm on your side and I always will be. You out of everyone should know that!"

Ryker proposed a question. "What if you get hurt?"

"I can protect myself. Besides, I'm sure whatever your issue is isn't as bad as you make it seem."

Despite all of Grayson's confidence in being right it was bad, very bad. Alexander was probably worse than Ryker was making him out to be right now and he couldn't just tell him why. The Sallow family combined was dreadful too, bringing pain to anyone who dared to cross them and their wishes. They would destroy Grayson and Ryker himself in a matter of minutes without even having to lay a hand on them. No amount of security systems, self defense classes, or safe houses could keep him from danger if it was found out he knew what was going on. Ryker couldn't risk that. Between Grayson's life and their friendship he would pick Grayson's life no matter what he had to sacrifice.

"Someone wants to ruin my job and reputation." Ryker caved in, leaving a small hole of breathing room for fabrication of a lie. "We aren't on the same side of everything and they were giving me two weeks."

"Two weeks?" Grayson sat up, twisting his body back towards Ryker. "That's why you wanted us to do something. Someone is trying to hurt you?"

Ryker nodded. "In a way."

A weight was added to Ryker's arm—a warm comforting hand, "So what are we doing here? We should be at home, so you can destroy them."

~~

One week was left. With all the adventures taken up within the first few days of the week—as well as the trip to the aquarium—Ryker was left with one week to plan. One week to make a choice on what he was going to be doing in the end. He made a truce with Alexander giving them both two weeks but how were they both using those two weeks? That was all that mattered in the end.

Ryker for one knew how he was going to spend his final week—preparing.

"Finding some good blackmail?"

Ryker glanced up from his laptop and towards his best friend who had entered the living room. Holding on tightly to his computer, he swung his legs off of the couch to give Grayson a chance to sit down but Grayson walked right by the seat and took one of the arm chairs in the room instead. Ryker rolled his eyes, pulling his legs back to lay across the couch and resituating his computer on his lap.

He had spent the first two days of his last week

going through every book and newspaper he could get his hands on cheaply—all items that now laid scattered around not only the living room but his bedroom and the dinning room. The only real information coming up from that was a recent wedding announcement that was floating around for the past few months in a multitude of papers—it was not new information. After he had gotten both annoyed and bored of the dusty and rough paper he had moved on to the internet. Of course he probably should have started here but it was a lot harder to delete or remove information from published papers and books than the internet. But nothing ever really gets deleted from the internet.

"First off, I'm totally not blackmailing anyone. Secondly, even if I was, that is illegal and if I told you I was then you would be an accessory to a crime." Ryker pointed out. Was Grayson wrong in the terms he used? No. But was he wrong to believe Ryker would admit to a crime in front of him? Absolutely.

Grayson stuck his tongue out. Kicking his legs over the arm of the chair, he slouched down using the couch more like a bed than a chair in the first place. He grabbed a black blanket from its folded spot on the chair back, pulling it off the back and over his legs.

"You say tom*a*to, I say tomat*o*, " Grayson waved his hand, like swiping away an irritating fly, to wave off the invisible words that flew towards him.

This was all coming from the student who actually took criminal justice during high school, was now acting like he was above the law and could make up his own sayings about how the law worked. Luckily, Ryker just happened to be involved in a job field that required him to know the basics of laws. Of course Grayson didn't know that but he wasn't meant to.

"That's a stupid quote and an even stupider way of thinking."

Ryker stared back down at his laptop and the paused video that was loaded upon it. A small huddled group was trying to move past a crowd of people that had formed around not only them but the vehicle they were supposed to be getting to leave their dreaded location they were currently stuck in. From Ryker's view it was saddening to watch the family having to push past those horrible people blocking, photographing, and recording them. Especially with the young girl that was being held by neither parents but instead a somewhat hooded boy trying to hide his identity.

"So," Grayson held out the last letter longer than needed. "How's your not blackmail search going?"

Ryker pressed the spacebar to let the video begin to play, the volume off and the captions were rendered useless with the multitude of yells and cries for answers to jumbled questions. It was just as frustrating listening to the incoherent words as it was to watch the captions go by with no idea what was being said. He had to pick his battles and decided this watch through to just watch the people moving on the screen.

"Fine."

Ryker frowned, scrolling through the suggested next video list below the one he had already fully watched. Grayson hummed in response, flipping on the TV to fill in

Ryker's soundless studies. He pulled one of the living room pillows close to his body curling around it as he looked in the direction of the screen where a cooking show played.

Just fine.

"You okay with me watching this?" Grayson gestured aimlessly towards the TV.

Ryker didn't bother to look up from his computer, scrolling through the next recommended videos laying there for him. "Go for it."

Ryker's frown quickly disappeared and was replaced with a smile as his cursor hovered over the title of a video with only a few views listed on it.

Sallow Corporation (Behind the scenes)

"Gottcha asshole."

~~

"Coffee?"

Ryker glanced up at his office door which had been pushed open by a lonely bartender. His request for a position behind the bar had been granted by the scheduling manager—the exact same manager who was working on the schedule for the next two weeks. Or was he?

"Bribing me to put you at the bar next week, Marc?" Ryker slid a manila folder across the table to hide the papers messily deposited on the desk. Smacking a few of the poking out edges in an attempt to get them under the folder as well.

"Maybe." Marc responded. "Is it working?"

Ryker groaned as he reached his hand out, moving

his fingers in and out like a child who wanted the item their parents currently held out of their grasp. Marc smirked, holding the warm cup of coffee out towards his boss.

"Why do I feel like you're not working on just the schedule?" Marc leaned against the wooden frame of the door, arms crossed while he peered at the bright computer which shone against Ryker's pale skin. Healing red contrasted against the light colors of his skin. Different injury coverings along his arms and leg from where he went crashing through a window.

"Why do you think I'm not?"

"Because if you were then you would be on your computer, everything is computerized now." Marc clicked his tongue, pushing away from the wall. "But I also feel like if you were doing something else it would be smart not to tell anyone. Leaving witnesses would be bad."

"I don't know what you could possibly be talking about." Ryker rocked back in his swivel chair. One leg on top of the other, arms crossed over his chest. His eyes narrowed, his voice becoming harsh with the next words that escaped him. "And if you did know something was up then I think it would be wise for you to shut your mouth."

"Sure thing, bossman."

Marc winked with a grin stretching from ear to ear, earning the largest eye roll from his manager, literally forcing Ryker's head to turn with its movement. The bartender scoffed, waving off his manager on his way out of the office so he could go finish his shift on the floor. He only had about an hour left. While he would love to waste it all he knew Ryker would have a fit if he did—their new hire was probably struggling with help so without help they were more than likely dying out there.

"Stop leaving the kid on the floor alone!" Was the last thing Ryker called out.

The restaurant manager rocked forward, swiveling to face his desk again. Pushing the manilla folder to the side once again a simple set of blueprints was laying on the desk. A frown emerged on Ryker's face again. Yellow highlights bled through the paper signifying every exit in the building but one. The exit that Ryker had taken a few days prior but for some reason he couldn't find it on the map. There was just one explanation—the exit didn't exist.

~~

Grayson would kill him if he knew about the abandoned film set Ryker found himself standing in front of. Three of the front windows had been shattered and graffiti clung to the walls with the life it was grante. It would have been a perfect disguise for a hideout if it was still being used that way—but it wasn't. Once a cover is blown there is no reason to stay.

That's why it was perfect.

That's why Ryker entered the unfinished multi-story building and walked through unbuilt halls just to enter a large room again. The last location Ryker fought Alexander inside of before Grayson's last accident. A car crash that happened so strangely close to the battle that Ryker hadn't fully expected. He knew the possibility with his own choices but that guaranteed nothing. So why did it seem like something wrong happened at exactly the right time?

Everything wrong was happening at the right time. The crash, the crowbar just sitting out so Ryker could escape, the police showing up, it all just happened so perfectly.

Ryker walked over to the table in the middle of the room. Ashes laid over damaged bits of paper. The crowbar was back in its place against the table, but Ryker hadn't put it back. He kicked it, listening to it clatter against the ground as he squatted down beside it. A tiny white X was tapped to the dusty ground.

"No!" Ryker exclaimed. His hand ran over the tap, peeling it from its spot on the ground and revealing the dark clean spot underneath. The floor was discolored, it had been there for a long time.

The exit hadn't been on the blue prints because it had been made as an escape from the police that someone had called. It had been left as the only path out of the building without fear of getting caught. A whole other hallway leading exactly where he was meant to be.

Ryker thought he had planned all of this out on his own, but Alexander had been ten steps ahead of him at all time. Now it was time for Ryker to skip over his plan. He needed to set a trap and he needed Alexander to walk straight into it.

~~

"Ooh can we get—"

"No." Ryker smacked the hand that reached out

towards a stone bee sculpture on one of the shelves making up the aisle they walked down. It was quickly pulled away and towards a frowning body next to him.

Sometimes Ryker hated shopping with Grayson. He always made it more difficult than it needed to be.

It had been less than a day since Ryker had ventured over to the film scene and he had not told Grayson about it. Grayson didn't need to know, he already knew too much anyways. No need to danger him further.

With the harsh wood, paint, and sawdust smell filling his nose, his head was starting to pound into a dull ache. He despised the smell, it wasn't something he ever found very pleasing yet it was more than necessary to gather the materials. Grayson causing trouble wasn't stopping his ever growing headache.

But Grayson pushing the cart they had making it slightly easier for Ryker to control the random items he threw into the cart. So while their spending wasn't so high, it didn't mean he stopped everything from magically falling inside. Amongst the list of items that would soon be making their home in the apartment included a clearance small skeleton, a rainbow welcome mat—wanting it just because Ryker touched it once—and two gray elephant bookends that made it seem like the legs of the animal were holding the books up.

"Aw." Grayson whined. He leaned forward on crossed arms which laid on top of the cart's handle. He wore his normal bright red sunglasses blocking Ryker's view of his eyes but he was sure that he was earning himself the sad puppy eyes right now.

"You don't need it!"

"But it's lonely, Alix!" Grayson shot up with his exclamation.

His excuse for getting anything even if he had no idea what it was in the first place. They had so many items in their house that Ryker knew they didn't need or ever use but it was because Grayson kept giving him that stupid excuse and he couldn't say no. "It needs friends and a home! Its name is Zom-Bee!"

Ryker scoffed, taking over the pushing of the gray cart from Grayson. He pointed towards the shelf as he continued to walk past it. "Put the stupid thing in the cart before I leave both you and it behind."

Grayson had a warm smile that formed on his face, clapping his hands together before he reached out and grabbed his prize for 'convincing' Ryker to let him get it. But to be honest Ryker didn't care because it was easier to get Grayson distracted then tell him about why he was dropping metal cylinders, a tool box, and wooden boards into the cart.

"I got a bee! I got a bee!" Grayson sang, skipping back towards the cart with his trophy in hand, placing it gently in the cart next to his other claimed items.

Great. Now I have to deal with this the rest of the trip, Ryker thought but he couldn't help but smile at his best friend and his excitement over such a small thing. He was happy he got to see these small things so close to what he knew wouldn't end up being so good when it happened.

There was so little time left to make Grayson as happy as possible with these little things and Ryker wasn't going to waste these chances. Yes, he was going to pretend to put up a little fight with it but in the end Grayson's items and wants would end up in the cart even if he wasn't looking that way when they went in.

While he had planned out what he thought would go down there was little time left and little guarantee for a one hundred percent success rate. So little time to make sure everything went perfectly. So little time to try and figure out how he was supposed to say goodbye.

~~

"Damn it!"

Ryker threw down the screwdriver he had been using. He was going to have to clean it later before the metal was ruined with his blood but for now he had something else to handle.

He pushed himself to his feet and slid them on the wooden boards the ground was made of as he walked towards the kitchen clutching one of his hands with his other. Little drips fell to the ground that he would have to clean up later.

Clear water from the faucet splashed down into the basin, swiftly dyed red with blood that flowed into the drain. Luckily none of the dishes had been inside the metal container and now getting dirty, Grayson had cleaned them earlier leaving that worry from Ryker's mind.

Ryker bit back the curses that wanted to escape from his lips and out into the opening. The cut on his hand, the one he wouldn't have had if it was holding his contraption properly, wasn't bad enough to need any advance care but it was just another injury to add with all the others he had. Most of his cuts and bruises from his last fight—and going through that window—had at least begun to heal and scar but this was just a new open wound. Another one he would have to either explain or lie to Grayson about.

He didn't like to lie to him.

"Gray, where's the first aid kit?" Ryker called out.

There wasn't an answer for a moment. Ryker would have thought that Grayson wasn't even in the apartment if he hadn't heard the slamming down the hallway containing only their two bedrooms, their bathroom, and a closet. A minute later Grayson waddled in his black pajama shirt and dinosaur pajama pants, standing out brightly was the white kit he held loosely in his hands.

"Dang it Alix, how did you get hurt this time?" Grayson tossed the first aid kit on the kitchen counter where he began to open it for Ryker's use.

"Screwdriver slipped." Ryker grumbled his answer, pulling out the items that had been made their home. "Which reminds me, I should warn you that tools are on the living room floor so be careful in there."

Grayson stuck his tongue out in response but didn't dare to step into the potentially dangerous room. Instead he decided to lean against the countertop as he *watched* Ryker bandage up his own hand.

"Eyes hurting?" Ryker questioned, gesturing aimlessly towards the bright sunglasses Grayson wore. It was unusual for him to wear them within the apartment without a major reason, typically being his eyes hurting him. It happened to be a simple way to change the topic as well.

"It's fine." Grayson responded. "How's your secret mission going?"

"Stop asking questions I'm not going to answer." Ryker responded. Grayson let out a scoff with the response that Ryker had given to him. He already learned what parts of the story Ryker wanted him to know.

"I can't be helpful if you don't tell me anything."

Ryker taped down the bandage on his hand. "Good because I don't want your help. This has nothing to do with you anyways, so don't try to get involved."

"I'm not going to get hurt, so there is no reason to worry Ryker."

Ryker tensed up upon hearing his full name being said by his best friend, despite having heard it come from his mouth many times before. He rarely ever gave up his special used nickname if it was anything good. He didn't like it, he didn't like any of it.

"Grayson, I can't let you get involved." Ryker stated. "I will be fine by myself."

The room fell into a moment of silence between the two roommates. He let out a sigh. "Please just promise me that you will stay out of trouble, and if you learn something you won't come around."

"What are you planning on doing that is making you this worried?" Grayson asked, but he knew he wouldn't get an answer from his best friend. "Ryker, how much trouble are you about to get into?"

Ryker walked away from the counter, grabbing a cloth that hung off the handle of their stove and began the process of cleaning the sink and counters of sprinkled drips of blood in silence. He didn't want to tell Grayson the full truth, he knew what he needed and nothing else. There was no reason to get a civilian involved in this.

"I know you don't want me to help, but I care about you. I just want you to be safe. Grayson ran his hands over the counters, grabbing the few items that had been left out by Ryker and shoved them back into the first aid kit. "You keep getting hurt and I'm afraid of you not coming back from this one."

Spinning on his heel, Ryker turned so his view laid on the other. "I'm not planning on leaving you, and even if I do you are more than capable of making new friends."

"Maybe I don't want new friends. It's difficult to get a new best friend." Grayson crossed his arms over his chest. Ryker chuckled at his response, walking over to finish the job Grayson had started but quit on. "So you better go and win whatever this is before coming back to me. Okay? Promise?"

"I promise to come back, Gray."

Grayson gently grabbed his friend's bandaged hand, laying a *'healing'* kiss on top of it—preparing it for the potential of battle it would have to go through with no idea how bad it could end up being. He looked up towards Ryker with a grin. "Good. Now go kick his ass."

Chapter 11

Everything was ready, Ryker was ready.

In a room set up with a row of old computers sat a taken up seat. A soft piano and violin duet came from the speakers on either side of the computer, filling up the silence of a mostly empty room. Nowadays it would be counted as old school technology but for some it was all they had but the venue on screen didn't seem to be doing any better.

Only two screens turned on—one with a paused video and the other with some sort of live stream playing. Right now people were just walking to find their seats, a photographer at the end of the aisle to get some pictures of the guests until the main part of the event began. Occasionally the photographer turned to take pictures of something off the screen before turning back towards the guests who all seemed to smile happily. Why would they not be happy? It was two people's wedding, it was a time to be happy for everyone.

And a long distance away the mood was sullen. It was far and safe away for the man that sat in his normal all black attire tinkering away at one of the many duplicated items that sat in a perfect row on a table. Just because it was safe for him didn't mean it was safe for others.

He hummed quietly to himself, occasionally speaking to no one but the items in his hand when they annoyed him with them. All until the music finally switched to a slower song.

A framed picture of mostly color was tapped, pushing it to be aligned next to the computers. Dust laid on the wood of the table but the picture shone with perfectly cleaned glass in front of it. A treasured item.

The camera for the streaming service turned, shifting the attention towards the gothic stone archway leading out of a building. The screens in the venue and the one on the computer were taken up by a little girl standing in the doorway. A long periwinkle dress covered her small body. A small basket held in her hands full of baby pink and white flower petals. Her blond —almost white— hair had been tugged back into braids that curled into a bun on the back of her head, full baby pink and white flowers braided into her hair.

Her little white heels tapped against the stone tile ground which was painted with the sun coming from the stained glass windows encompassing the walls of the church.

"Go on Olivia." Static came through the speakers with a harsh bodiless voice following. They were hushed voices, almost too obvious it wasn't supposed to be heard. Olivia glanced back into the archway, a hand peaked out behind the girl waving her on. "Come on, go to your brother."

Olivia beamed, jumping before starting skipping down the aisle to the front. Occasionally her hand went into the basket she held and allowed little petals flutter to the ground. Her flower sandals caused her to stumble but by the point of her making it to the end of the aisle she was still beaming—especially when she ran towards a man in a suit, standing there waiting.

"Alexander!" She dropped her basket, running to him and wrapping her arms around him. He chuckled, lifting her off the ground for a momentary hug. Placing her back on the ground he brushed a loose strand of hair from her face. Someone from the audience pulled the basket to clear it from the aisle.

"Hey Livie, can you go stand with mom please?"

A scoff came from the craftsman who watched it from the chair he spun in. He spun an unused safety clip on his fingers. His eyes narrowed, landing on the screens in front of him. He pushed his feet against the ground rolling his chair to a further screen but his eyes never left the screaming video.

Soft classical music began to play. The traditional tune used in so many movies and TV shows for their wedding scenes.

The previous sound of guests had now fallen into

silence, heads turning towards a woman who moved into the archway. She stopped, staring down the aisle in a light gold lace a-line dress with her own white flower bouquet in her hands. Her red lips pressed together in a tight smile, squeezing her hands around the bouquet.

"Here comes the bride. Here comes the bride." The mocking sung words echoed in the large room. Hands waved in the air conducting the music wrong. but it was knowingly wrong, without care about the actual beat of the music.

No way she is happy.

The music came to a halt once the bride reached the end of the aisle, stepping up onto the platform where her groom, their friends, and the officiant all stood waiting for her. The groom rocked on his feet, a smile laid like a sticker on his face. Once on the stand the bride handed off her bouquet to her maid of honor before turning her head to look at her groom, a silent indication that the officiant could start his long speech of sorts.

"Good afternoon, family and friends. We have come here today to celebrate the wedding of Alexander Sallow and..."

Wheels screeched against stone ground that they should not have ever been put on top of. A grumble escaped the chair's current rider, rubbing behind his ears momentarily with the dreadful noise. Placed harshly on the ground his feet told the chair to stop him from rolling away from the computer he needed to access. A video loaded on the screen was already pulled up for him.

"Sorry Mr. Sallow, I'm cutting off your truce."

Ryker Griffin spoke pressing a bold red **STREAM** button. An unseen shrug left him. "Oh, and I need your screens."

He pressed the play button and allowed the beginning to start playing as a black screen, not only on his screens but the multitude of screens set up around the wedding venue held the video. It took a moment for any of the guests to notice but when a voice started and the first turned their head the others did as well.

"Truth. Are we all living the truth? Reality or a lie?" Scratchy, a deep voice shook the speakers on the table. Ryker leaned back watching black brighten into blurry moving video, a man stood in front of the camera he probably didn't even know was there. But even if he did, would he have let up his angered stance with a binder of weekly reports in his hand that was not curled into a fist?

"What the hell were you thinking?!" The man yelled at someone who was positioned outside of the shaking camera's view. "You could have just messed everything up for us because of a stupid crush!"

"I was being strategic." Someone, more than likely the one getting yelled at, off screen spoke. Their voice quivered with the words they tried to make bold and brave. Perhaps it could have been believable if that was the person the video was pointed at but he was not. "Having someone in that field that knows and likes us just gives us another string for business."

Ryker watched the crowd of the wedding jump when the binder was thrown off screen. A few people panicked to switch off the venue's screens with those horrible videos all while Alexander Sallow remained frozen, watching.

"We run the restaurant! We don't need another string!"

The video switched to a different one and once again the crowd was punished to watch every little piece of evidence of the behind the scenes Sallow family. Maybe that is why it was hidden so deeply on the internet. One day the Sallow family would have to learn that while they can try to force people not to watch something they can't get rid of everything.

"Turn those off!" Ryker smiled at Alexander's commanding voice which came through the second set of speakers. "Someone turn it off!"

Finally, Ryker shifted forward in his seat, reaching to grab an item in the shadows he revealed an intercom microphone. He leaned close to it and pressed the speak button. "Not every story ends with a happily ever after. So welcome world to the end and the official unveiling of the *real* Sallow family's life and understand why they are freaking out now. Everyone, meet the villains of the world."

~~

It hadn't taken long for the Sallow company to figure out how someone was watching and controlling their screens. But when they couldn't shut him out *everyone* got to see the violence with a silver post—previously holding up the ropes around the venue—meeting the brand new computer screens that had been set up for the occasion.

The old style tech was once in pristine condition now set in shattered piles which the Sallow company was more then okay paying for, or at least Ryker believed so. His camera had been cut off in the middle of watching Alexander's destruction of the multitude of television sets and himself. Ryker didn't even have to do much, he just gave Alexander a little nudge in the *right* direction.

Step one complete. Ryker thought to himself. Glancing to his right there were handheld machines he deposited earlier on the ground to wait their time. *Ready for you step two.*

Ryker hoisted himself up to his feet before a noise rang out through the building. It was his phone, but why was it going off? Who could possibly be calling him at this time? Grayson had said he would not be completely available—he would be if it was an emergency—and he wasn't on shift.

Curious, he pulled his phone from his pocket revealing the call ID.

Grayson

"Strange." Ryker mumbled. Grayson was supposed to be busy right now, but that didn't mean it was impossible for him to be calling. Pressing the green button he raised the phone to his ear expecting to hear the cheerful voice of his best friend. "Gray—"

"Hello, Ryker."

"Hey Ryker, I heard of this new cafe that just opened up and I think I'm going to go there. You know, while you do your not blackmailing."

"Oh, cool. I'll have my phone, text or call if you need anything."

A shiver shot up his spine, goosebumps rising along his arms and to where the hair stood up on the back of his neck. He took a deep breath before offering up a response. "Hello, Alexander."

"Oh come on you came to my wedding, I think we can be a little less formal *Alix*."

His hand turned a ghostly white as he gripped his phone. Ignoring Alexander's comment he asked, "Why do you have Grayson's phone? Where is he? What did you do to him?"

"None of that is something you should be worrying about right now. If it eases your mind to know he is safe, for now." Alexander responded. There was no way he didn't know how much Ryker hated that answer.

Ryker went quiet though on his end in an attempt to listen to the other side. Cars were beeping, mumbles of talk barely heard over Alexander's talking. No sounds or words of distress were coming with panic. Alexander couldn't be making a big scene right now so Grayson couldn't be in immediate danger.

"Instead why don't we talk about my wedding."

Nothing about the sounds told Ryker where Alexander might be other than he was standing in a public place and Grayson had to be nearby. If he had Grayson then there was no way he would let Grayson leave his grasp or range of grasp. Where was Grayson?

"What do you want?" Ryker snapped.

"Just to talk. Mutual location, bunch of witnesses, you know the works."

Ryker sat back in his seat that he hadn't been able to step away from, pulling a small stack of sticky notes towards him to write down the address that Alexander was going to give him. "Fine, but you have to leave Grayson alone. You can't even lay a hand on him. Okay?"

"Oh Ryker—"

"Promise me!" Ryker yelled. A loud bang echoed through the warehouse upon the contact of Ryker's hand against this wooden desk he sat at.

Alexander released a chuckle. "Fine. I promise."

"Okay, so where do I meet you?"

Ryker debated asking the question again with the silence that came over the call. Wondering if Alexander was even still on the other side of the phone.

"Myst Falls, 6pm."

Ryker wrapped his spare hand around a pen, hovering it over the sticky note he was going to write on. He took a deep breath before giving Alexander a soft okay. Ryker gently placed his phone down, tapping it with his now empty hand.

"Breathe." Ryker spoke to himself, wishing for it to be a different voice gliding through his ears and speaking than his own. Some joking high pitched voice, or a rumbling low one he sometimes used, but neither came out. His hand shook, pressing one against the cold wooden desk to get to his feet and the other was still holding his pen but now in a more shaking grasp. "Just breathe."

Screw breathing.

Ryker lifted his arm, slamming the end of the pen into his stick notes. Once.. twice.. After the third time he let the pen fall broken on to the desk. He cracked his knuckles, spinning away from the desk.

"I'm done playing nice." Ryker snapped. His eyes landed on his bag waiting around for him and the next step of his plans. A large grin crept up his face. "This is ending. Today."

~~

Ryker didn't bother to dress out of his cargo pants and bomber jacket before the quick—breaking every speed limit—drive to the restaurant. He barely got his car properly in his labeled spot. The **MANAGER** spot. He climbed out of his car, striding towards the building and pushing past the small line at the door to enter.

"Ryker? Thank god, you're here." Marc scrambled towards the door, dropping the schedule book on the host desk and abandoning the person on host shift there to handle the line. Ryker scanned the room for any signs of that stuck up polished face his fists begged to get near that perfect fake smile.Maybe if he could just break that straight nose from its place.

"We were about to call you." Marc continued. "Briar is late and she isn't answering her phone. The Sallow family secretary just called—"

"Which table?" Ryker cut in. He didn't care about the other missing manager or even the line that was starting out of the door, everything that happened here happened for a reason.. "Which table did you put him at?"

"Back right booth." Marc answered. "The back and a booth was all that was requested. I know they don't like being near the windows either."

Ryker nodded, starting off in that direction until Marc called out after him. "What are you doing?"

"Preparing for my meeting with Mr. Sallow."

"Ryker." He turned back towards his employee. Marc gestured up towards the TV's that were playing a station he never believed he would see—the news. "They asked for it to be playing."

People ran across the screen, muted screams were able to be seen by the heads that had turned to look at the multitude of screens. Fire erupted, spreading along the floor and walls, chasing after the scared civilians. It showed terror and destruction but along the bottom were fast moving words but Ryker caught enough of them to figure out what was being said.

National Hero putting a stop to the terrorist group known as—

"What do you want me to do, boss?" Marc asked.

Ryker let out a chuckle, waving off the TVs like they would move from where they screwed into stands on the walls and ceilings. "Keep it on and do me a favor and go turn off the restaurant cameras."

"What?"

"You heard me, turn them off. The Sallows love their privacy and no camera on them so let's give them what that always want. Plans are going out the window and I guess that means we are making this up as we go." Ryker stated. He continued to walk towards the prepared table. "Myst Falls is preparing for a special guest, let's pull out all the stops. Make him feel at home, after all it was his wedding day. Let's give him a party."

~~

The restaurant ran quietly, only faint conversations came between members of families and the employees who were having to talk with the customers. People sat down in their seats and waited on quickly like normal but the tension in the room was so thick the diners could cut through it with their steak knives. The occasional frequent visitor had turned their heads to see their friendly manager sitting in a booth, tapping the edge of his butter knife against the wooden grain of the table digging into the design. Chips of wood had eventually started to break off of the edge but he didn't stop.

Tables had been rearranged, giving a lot of empty space near some of the booths, with a lot of the restaurant's normal set up that had not changed since Ryker joined the staff as a server. The curtains on every window had been drawn back giving full access to the view of the outside but also gave passing civilians a view inside.

A bell rang out into the restaurant. Heads snapped towards the door where a man stood. His hands moved to wipe down the wrinkles of the perfectly snug fitting suit he was wearing, his hair slicked back and not a single spot of his previous rage laid on him—except the beginnings of bruising on his knuckles—while he waited at the host stand.

Ryker spotted Marc staring at the front entrance while one of their younger hosts, a teenage boy named Zayn, moved towards the door.

"He.. hello. Your table is already set up. Right this way Mr. Sallow." Zayn gestured into the restaurant before moving ahead and towards the booth set up from the Sallow heir. Alexander strolled behind the kid, a smirk sitting on his face until he reached the table Ryker waited at.

"This isn't the table I requested." Alexander slid into the empty seat, his smirk fading rapidly. Ryker beamed at the new arrival though.

"Yeah well we were a little busy and that seat was taken." Ryker responded. Leaning in his seat to see the empty table that Alexander had previously requested. "We can't make everything work out for you."

"Well I hope you are prepared to try anyways." Plastic thudded softly against the table. Ryker watched a lime green flash drive bounce its way across the table and towards his rolled silverware. He just scoffed as Alexander continued to talk. "We need to talk—"

Alexander was cut off though when a glass clinked against the table. His head turned so his eyes would land on the bartender who dared to interrupt them with a large smile and a second drink in hand.

"Drinks from the bar. I said you were in a business meeting but a pretty lady wanted you to have them."

Both Ryker and Alexander turned their heads to the almost completely empty bar. At least he had the guts to back up the words that left his mouth even if it was a blatant lie.

"Thank you." Ryker spoke up. Marc gave a sharp nod, holding out the glass towards his manager as well as a napkin. Ryker responded with a nod, taking the items. "Back to work Marc."

Marc spun on his heel, speed walking away to leave the two alone with their *business meeting* to attend to still. Ryker sipped at his drink, placing down his *white* napkin. A smirk forming on his face.

"Is this really your plan?" Alexander questioned. Ryker's head tilted at the accusation coming. "Getting me drunk?"

"No."

"Really? Because that is what it looks like." Alexander pushed the glass forward with the knuckles of his hands.

Ryker reached forward to grab the drink from him, pushing himself to his feet. "Fine then, I'll just go and return it to the bar."

Ryker had gotten just a few steps away from the table when he felt something cold and metal get pushed into his lower back. The heat of breath hit his bare neck when Alexander leaned close to him, placing a harsh but stabilizing hand on his shoulder.

"You think I don't know what you are doing?" Alexander dug the gun into Ryker's back. "I'm not stupid but I'm sure you know that already."

"Oh I'm very much aware." Ryker tilted his head back to look at Alexander. An unnatural smile landing on his face. "But maybe you shouldn't act like you are."

Ryker pointed towards the window they happened to be standing right in front of getting Alexander to turn his head to face the crowd of people that had begun to form there with large flashing cameras in hand. All of them were facing the pair, but Alexander's weapon was just barely out of their line of sight. One wrong move and everyone would see.

A scoff rang out in Ryker's ears before the harsh grip on his shoulder let up, the hand slid across his shoulders so his arm went behind the boy. The gun—still pressed firmly into his skin—slid along his back to his side where Alexander could block it with his own body. At the same time he blocked the flashing lights from the cameras leaving their shadows on the wall.

"Smile and don't make a scene." Alexander whispered.

Coughing filled what had become a quick silence. Ryker tilted his head up towards the TV's which were still playing. He slowly raised his hand, waving at it with his fingers. "Say hi."

Ryker waited until Alexander lifted his head to face the blank screens before swinging his arm back straight into Alexander's face. Listening to the satisfying crack, distorting the nose bone from its natural state. He didn't even try to stop the loud horrible cackle that escaped from his mouth, watching Alexander stumble away with his hands covering his nose.

All the pain he probably felt because he was stupid enough to look at the blank TV screens. The news was long turned off before the Sallow paparazzi and Alexander had even arrived. He reached down and pulled a metal object from its home in a holster hidden beneath his bomber jacket.

Diners screamed, jumping up at the sight of the weapon.
Alexander stood up straight, matching eye contact with his current enemy at the time. He stood up straighter as he stared at the end of a gun's barrel.

"Decided to take a gun to a gun fight this time. Wise, don't you think Alex?"

"Do you think it is wise to pull your gun in front of cameras?"

Ryker nodded. He tilted his head, looking out the now empty window. Alexander's eyes widened at the sight. "Actually yeah, especially because they aren't your real paparazzi."

Ryker looked at Alexander again, keeping his gun raised while he took a few small steps forward. A grin laid on his face while he looked at his current enemy. Of course he too was face to face with the barrel of a gun, but unlike Alexander he wasn't scared or at least he didn't want to look so.

"This ends today." Ryker snapped.

"Yeah it does!"

Metal clattered to the ground, smoke rising off the ending of one item. A gasped out 'No' was barely uncovered because of the running and scrambling of the terrified diners. Two became three in the middle of the restaurant, one who was never supposed to be there and was safe in their spot behind the counter before.

Ryker took a small step forward, holding his arms out until weight fell into them. Quickly, he lowered himself and the body against him to the ground. His shaking hands moved towards red liquid staining the required white uniform.

"Hey, it's going to be okay." Ryker spoke. Shoes clacked against the ground, stepping away from them until it disappeared completely. "Marc, you're going to be okay."

"Sorry boss." Marc smiled up at Ryker. His face contorted with pain as Ryker pressed his hand against the oozing wound. The dirty factor made him want to squirm but he kept the pressure instead. "I guess the pretty lady didn't plan this out well."

Ryker bit down on his lip. "The pretty lady can shut up. You're going to be okay."

"No it's not and you know it." Marc answered. "I don't know what's going on but you better win. So go."

"Marc—" Sirens rang out from outside. Ryker's head snapped towards the front of the building which was no longer filled with the previously freaking out diners. Police were coming, someone had called them.

"Go."

Ryker let out a curse, tugging his jacket off. He placed the bartender's hand over his own injury before laying the jacket over him. "Police are coming and I'm sure an ambulance is too. So put pressure, and you better live. I can't be losing my best bartender. I would be stuck with Sofi."

"Make no promises, break no hearts."

Ryker used his sleeve to wipe away '*dirt from his eyes*'. Yeah there was just something in his eyes, that was it. He took a deep breath, getting to his feet and turning away from the bartender he wouldn't hesitate to claim as his favorite. He scooped his gun off the ground before heading towards the only exit Alexander could have taken out of the now empty restaurant.

He walked through the usually roaring and disorderly kitchen that had fallen into a state of weird tranquility. It was wrong. All of it was so wrong.

A required exit door sat on the other side of the kitchen and not to Ryker's surprise it was swinging shut. He was closing in very quickly. So he picked up his pace, slamming the door open and let him get hit by the harsh wind outside. Attempting to flee the scene was the suit wearing Sallow child.

"Alexander!" Ryker yelled. He pointed the gun into the air, pulling the trigger so the weapon let out a loud bang. Alexander turned to face him, his hands empty of a weapon which still laid on the tilted floor of the restaurant's dining area. His hands went up into the air while Ryker swiftly closed the distance.

"You just killed my friend." Ryker snapped.

"I didn't—"

Alexander was cut off when a fist made contact with his face, causing him to stumble back with what was probably his already aching nose. He didn't get to his feet before Ryker lifted his legs, kicking the Sallow heir off balance where he fell and went crashing to the muddy ground.

Even if the ambulance could arrive soon—the sirens had gone quiet—the chances of Marc making it through slimmed every moment he was away from a hospital. And the chances of Ryker being able to make it home to Grayson vanished too. His friend was dying and his best friend was going to be alone. Alexander had to pay.

"Ry—"

He wasn't even given a chance to finish his words, Ryker was on top of him in a matter of seconds swinging his fists. Each hit colliding right against the stupid perfectly constructed skull of the Sallow legacy beneath him. His fist ached more and more with each hit, a warm liquid getting splattered on his skin, but he kept hitting. And hitting... And hitting...

He was going to kill him.

Even as Alexander tried to lift his hands to block his face Ryker kept going. All he could see was *red* until he literally saw red and white and blue.

"Police! Put your hands in the air!"

With a fist already raised Ryker froze in his place with the noises of clicks and feet squelching against the muddy ground. He pushed himself up to his feet, spinning on the squishy ground. His hands raised to be above his head while guns were trained on him alone.

His whole body tensed up upon hearing a cough from behind him as he knew who got up. A rough grip came to one of his hands as it was forced behind him. Warm breath landed on the back of his neck, goosebumps forming while the hair on the back of his neck stood up.

But all Ryker could look at was a black car that

had pulled up into the grass, it wasn't one of the police ones that were parked on the in view sidewalk. His chest tightened as he stared towards bright red sunglasses.

"Ryker Griffin, you are under arrest for the distribution of government documents to the public, interfering with government sanctioned missions, assault of a government official, *and* the murder of Marc Reed." Alexander spoke. Ryker tilted his head to watch an officer move towards a weapon that still laid on the ground, his weapon. The only one that had been fired twice. The only one with any actual bullets inside of it.

Cold metal wrapped around Ryker's wrists behind him, a soft metallic click came with the tightening metal. He turned his head back towards the person who had walked until one of the officers stopped him.

"You have the right to remain silent, anything you say can and will be used against you in a court of law.."

Ryker was pushed to start walking. Start walking towards the police cars by the road and to start walking towards him. Towards—

"Grayson." Ryker called out, only for his best friend to turn his head away from him. He wanted to stop, call out to Grayson, but Alexander pushed him to keep him walking to the cars. He didn't want to continue, he wanted to see Grayson and beg for him to just say anything.

When they reached the car Alexander opened the door, giving a small gesture for Ryker to get in willingly before it happened unwillingly. Ryker looked past Alexander one last time towards that black car but got into the car without another fight—Alexander's bloody face already being a sign that he could win if the ground was fair anyways.

"Who's the villain now, Ryker?"

FILE NAME : IT'S OVER

December 10 2065

Dear Grayson

A Final Goodbye
Take 18

00:00:00 –> 00:00:02
- Is this thing working?

00:00:04 –> 00:00:05
[Keyboard click]

00:00:07 –> 00:00:16
- Hello Grayson. I'm going to start
this by saying this is not an apology
video so if that is what you wanted then
I would suggest turning this video off
and waiting for another time.

00:00:18 –> 00:00:23
- If you aren't Grayson and
watching this then stop, this isn't
for you and this isn't any kind of
confession.

00:00:25 –> 00:00:26
[Sigh]

00:00:28 –> 00:00:42

- I knew what I was doing the whole time so don't let someone try to convince you otherwise. They will try to tell you they are right and they have the truth about everything, don't believe them. I just wanted to save the world. I wanted to save you.

00:00:42 -> 00:00:44
[Loud Groan]
[Hand slams against table]

00:00:46 -> 00:01:00
- I guess that doesn't explain why though.

Why I was sneaking out at night, why I was lying to you, why I was hurting you to keep you safe. But I don't know if I can ever explain it in a way you will understand. I can try though.

00:01:02 -> 00:01:25
- It started when you had your accident and ever since then I've been mad. For a while now I thought I was mad at the universe. Blaming it for everything that happened to your sister, your family, and most importantly you. I thought I was mad at the world. But

maybe I was just mad at myself. Mad that I watched you get hurt and I was useless. Mad that for once I couldn't do anything.

00:01:27 —> 00:01:40
[Scoff]
- You were hurt and I hated to see you like that and I didn't want to see anyone else in that position. I didn't want to see anyone else lose something or someone. Too many people have lost things to this world.

00:01:41 —> 00:01:43
[Sigh]

00:01:44 —> 00:02:10
I wanted the universe to change. But it seems that in an attempt to stop people from being hurt I ended up being a large cause of their pain. It's too late to stop though and the biggest source of pain in the world comes from the Sallow Corporation. They run everything, trying to monopolize the world, controlling what happens and forcing everyone to fall into their standards.

Charlotte and Julian Sallow have

ruined this world and tomorrow I plan to
stop them.

        00:02:13 -> 00:02:20
    - I think I might go down with them
though and that would leave you alone,
which I am...

        00:02:20 -> 00:02:31
    [Soft chuckle]
    - Oh, I guess this is an apology
video.
    I'm sorry Grayson.
    I'm sorry for never telling you the
truth about what was going on and lying
to you every time you asked.
    I'm-

        00:02:32 -> 00:02:47
    [Door creaks out]
    - {Grayson} Hey, Alix, what's
taking so long? I thought you said we
were going shopping.
    - {Ryker} Yeah we are, I'll be
right there just give me three minutes.
    - {Grayson} Okay.

        00:02:49 -> 00:02:51
    [Door slams shut]
    [Chair squeaks]

00:02:53 --> 00:03:03
- Sorry, where was I?
Oh yeah apologizing in the not
apology video.
[Laugh] Guess it is just like the
totally not blackmailing.

00:03:05 --> 00:03:25
[Clearing throat]
- Anyways, I'm sorry. I never
wanted you to get hurt or involved and
I know if you are watching this you
probably got pulled in somehow.
I promise this was nothing other
than me trying to keep you and the world
safe.
Something inside me just broke when
I saw you in that hospital bed I think.
I just wanted to make sure the world was
a better place for you.

00:03:27 --> 00:03:32
[Sniffle]
[Voice cracking up]
- I don't regret anything I did,
except never telling you.

00:03:38 --> 00:03:40
- Goodbye.

Epilogue

Time passed and Ryker had found himself sentenced to a life of orange jumpsuits and constant time behind metal bars. He didn't care to put up a fight either as he was stuck listening to a stupid attorney trying to argue for him—he didn't pay for one though. Where did it come from? He didn't have the money to afford a good one yet Ryker knew this wasn't one appointed to him. He had seen this guy somewhere before, he was good and he cost good money. Who would have bought him an attorney.

But it didn't matter how good someone was at their job or how many cases they had won that everyone else seemed impossible. No matter how much they tried to argue they all knew he was guilty, everyone knew he was guilty. *He* knew he was guilty.

And Ryker knew Grayson never came to the trial.

He didn't come during his time sitting in a cell and make every promise he knew that it would be okay in the end. Or even try to fight for the bail which Ryker wasn't given the option of. He didn't dress up in his finest suit and come to court to testify for his best friends' innocents until he was crying on the stand. He didn't even accept Ryker's one phone call to him. The only phone called Ryker even wanted to make to the only person he ever really cared about that was still alive.

The one person that could have been expected to come to the trial never did, and Ryker didn't want him to have come either.

~~

It was a cold winter day when a black car pulled up in front of the closest prison to the city. It was the only thing requested as part of the sentencing. It was likely the only thing they were willing to give to him.

The wind blew harshly sparking goosebumps to form on all who dared to exit into the outside world. But someone did dare to do that, bundled up in the giant fire hydrant red jacket they pulled out of the bottom of his closet and a set of matching monster hat and gloves—the monster ate his fingers when he turned them into mittens with the attachable piece.

Recently cut copper hair barely stuck out of the edge of the hat, swaying with the wind against it. The bundled up boy waddled towards the prison. Holding one of his hands close to his body for warmth while the other had to brave the cold for the white cane he held out as a guide. He could lose one hand to the hold, not both.

Someone who was leaving held the door open for him just getting him stopped instantly by a uniformed man waiting in the first room of entrance. "Are you here to visit someone?"

"Yeah, Ryker Alix Griffin and it is scheduled already." He was already working on pulling his coat off with the knowledge he would have to shove it into a locker. The only item that would have to go in, he had left everything else behind except the things he was bringing with him. "My name is Grayson Finch."

The prison guard nodded, and while Grayson

couldn't see the response he smiled. All while the guard offered to help him sign in and get through security. The whole time he just kept smiling all the way to a watched door.

Security went surprisingly quick, the longest part was the second look over of the small document that he had brought with him. A document that was preapproved when scheduling his visit in the first place but they decided needed to be looked over again.

Whatever pleased them and let this go faster. Could it just go faster?

"Thank you." Grayson spoke walking through the held open door and into a dull large room that had been divided with glass and the counter it sat on. Phones—which had no real use but most people pretended they did—sat on dividers, a few of the spots already taken up by people on either side.

Taking a deep breath, he willed himself to continue out of the doorway and forward where the guard at the door had instructed him there was an empty chair. Lucky for him, right?

What was luck?

A horrible screech was released from the chair he grabbed sliding across the stone ground. Grayson slipped into the chair in what seemed to be a freezing room, now waiting. For seconds, maybe minutes, or even hours. He had no way to tell except for the annoying ticking of a clock behind him somewhere. There was no point glancing back at something that would be unhelpful. If he did he guessed he would just throw the pen in his hand at it just to try and get it to shut up. Even though it was incredibly obnoxious it was the only thing other than people talking telling him he was really here. Besides, his aim was horrible as a kid so he was sure it would be even worse now. So he just placed his hands on the counter in front of him.

A set of doors somewhere creaked open with a loud, scratchy, voice, "I said I'm going!"

Grayson's chest tightened as footsteps echoed his way. Multiple guards had to have walked in with the amount of different footsteps that had been added even as he tried to listen in. Another chair scratched against the stone with the jingling of metal. A grinning person had taken place on the other side of the glass from him.

"You look shocked, Gray, and you were the one that came here." Ryker's voice rang through Grayson's ears like it had so many days in a row. At least this time it was all real, not recorded and not made up in his imagination. He was being spoken to. "After you ignored my first couple of phone calls I didn't think you would ever come."

"I didn't think I would either." Grayson responded. His hand reaching out, fingertips brushing against cold plastic. They slowly worked to pry the loops away from each other so his fingers could snake between them. Pulling away occasionally just to let the loops fall back together and ruining all that hard work.

"Hey, what's wrong?" Ryker asked.

"You. This situation you are in." Grayson stated. He bit down on his lip. The corners of his mouth tipping down. "It is not right, you were trying to save the world from people who were actually trying to hurt it. Who gets to determine what's right and wrong? Determine that what you did was wrong? Now who is supposed to save everyone?"

"Those aren't even your own words. I guess you never forgot anything from your theater classes," Ryker let out a breathy chuckle, stopping Grayson from continuing on. "You didn't come to give me a sob story did you?"

Grayson rolled his eyes, his frown disappearing in a heartbeat. "Of course not. I need you to sign some papers."

A guard moved forward and dropped a stack in front of the inmate. Already approved by members of the staff, Ryker was *gifted* with a pen to sign the documents Grayson had handed over at the security check.

"Oh thank you so very much." Ryker scoffed at the guard. The papers fluttered while being flipped through. "What is this?"

"Proper documents. You're signing permission to take your name off the apartment's lease."

Grayson clicked his own pen. A set of clicks and holdings, eight different clicks spread out into three sets of patterns before starting again. Or maybe it was just an overthought idea. It was nothing as Ryker clicked his own pen to sign one of the first blank lines on the pages.

"So, what's the plan now?" Ryker asked. He flipped through the pages to find any more of the lines he may need to sign. Closing the packet at the end he slammed the pen down for the still close by guard to take away. It was so fast, Grayson barely heard him move.

"So you have a plan all alone? Looks like that's

what you are saying, ready to be alone and going solo. What are you going to do now, Grayson?"

Grayson pushed himself to his feet. He lifted his hand and pressed it against the glass. "I'm going to tell you to shut up and run."

"What?"

"You'll figure it out."

Grayson turned on his heels and walked towards the door on his way out of the building. He tried to smile at every worker in the places he assumed they were. Just as he was about to reach the door he dropped his pen and raised his hands to cover his ears.

Yells and alarms started to ring through the building following a loud boom. Guards and other members of the jail jumped to their feet, running back towards the visiting and cell areas of the jail, calling out for no one to move. But Grayson was already gone and he wasn't planning on going back.

~~

"Took you long enough."

Grayson instinctively reached out for a hand to help him into the back area of a large black—or so he was told—van which pulled up in front of him. After months he still did it, even with no one to grab his hand like he expected. But this time his hand was met with warmth which wrapped around his hand, tugging him in. No metal clinked together making that terrible noise as he was pulled into the van.

The seats had been removed from the back area but it was probably safer that those in the back weren't easily seen by being buckled in. There were some areas to grasp along the edges anyways.

"Alix?"

"What's going on Grayson?" Ryker asked. Even though Grayson was in the car Ryker didn't let go of his hand.

The van—previously running for warmth—was turned off, the driver climbed out at some point during Grayson's arrival. Their exit provided a little extra privacy but took away comfortability and the safety of knowing everyone's location. Grayson himself would rather know where people were but he gave this one a pass.

Grayson pulled his hands from Ryker's grasp, "You were right, those weren't my words."

"Are you two done having your love reunion moment?"

Grayson turned around *looking* at the ally he had brought with him on this mission of a jailbreak. Ryker had grabbed his hand again, squeezing it tightly as he probably got a view of the hooded person standing there.

"Really? You are doing this right now?" Grayson scoffed at poor timing. Poor timing which was probably timed out perfectly.

"Alexander?" Ryker asked. "What the hell is going on here?"

Grayson forced his irritation away and beamed at his best friend with the offer of a change of topic. "We're leaving and you are going to teach us how to help you.

Both of us."

"What my parents do isn't right." Alexander spoke up. "Let's fix their mistakes."

Jasmine Martin is the best selling author of the story *To Define Us*—at least hopefully. She is a student at a Fine and Performing Arts High School and intends to continue her writing journey through college and into the far future.

She's published multiple pieces of her writing in *Siren* and *The Megalodon*. She lives in Northern Virginia, loves ghost stories and adventures. She wants to spread her love through her writing for all to enjoy.

More can be found at :
Tiktok @todefineusbook

www.ingramcontent.com/pod-product-compliance
Lightning Source LLC
Chambersburg PA
CBHW061449210726
48287CB00007B/2434